THEY FOU
WAY TO

BARBARA CARTLAND

Barbaracartland.com Ltd

.com

POD Preparation by M-Y Books
m-ybooks.co.uk

THE BARBARA CARTLAND PINK COLLECTION

Barbara Cartland was the most prolific bestselling author in the history of the world. She was frequently in the Guinness Book of Records for writing more books in a year than any other living author. In fact her most amazing literary feat was when her publishers asked for more Barbara Cartland romances, she doubled her output from 10 books a year to over 20 books a year, when she was 77.

She went on writing continuously at this rate for 20 years and wrote her last book at the age of 97, thus completing 400 books between the ages of 77 and 97.

Her publishers finally could not keep up with this phenomenal output, so at her death she left 160 unpublished manuscripts, something again that no other author has ever achieved.

Now the exciting news is that these 160 original unpublished Barbara Cartland books are ready for publication and they will be published by Barbaracartland.com exclusively on the internet, as the web is the best possible way to reach so many Barbara Cartland readers around the world.

The 160 books will be published monthly and will be numbered in sequence.

The series is called the Pink Collection as a tribute to Barbara Cartland whose favourite colour was pink and it became very much her trademark over the years.

The Barbara Cartland Pink Collection is published only on the internet. Log on to www.barbaracartland.com to find out how you can purchase the books monthly as they are published, and take out a subscription that will ensure that all subsequent editions are delivered to you by mail order to your home.

TITLES IN THIS SERIES

THE LATE DAME BARBARA CARTLAND

Barbara Cartland, who sadly died in May 2000 at the grand age of ninety eight, remains one of the world's most famous romantic novelists. With worldwide sales of over one billion, her outstanding 723 books have been translated into thirty six different languages, to be enjoyed by readers of romance globally.

Writing her first book "Jigsaw" at the age of 21, Barbara became an immediate bestseller. Building upon this initial success, she wrote continuously throughout her life, producing bestsellers for an astonishing 76 years. In addition to Barbara Cartland's legion of fans in the UK and across Europe, her books have always been immensely popular in the USA. In 1976 she achieved the unprecedented feat of having books at numbers 1 & 2 in the prestigious B. Dalton Bookseller bestsellers list.

Although she is often referred to as the "Queen of Romance", Barbara Cartland also wrote several historical biographies, six autobiographies and numerous theatrical plays as well as books on life, love, health and cookery. Becoming one of Britain's most popular media personalities and dressed in her trademark pink, Barbara spoke on radio and television about social and political issues, as well as making many public appearances.

In 1991 she became a Dame of the Order of the British Empire for her contribution to literature and her work for humanitarian and charitable causes.

Known for her glamour, style, and vitality Barbara Cartland became a legend in her own lifetime. Best remembered for her wonderful romantic novels and loved by millions of readers worldwide, her books remain treasured for their heroic heroes, plucky heroines and traditional values. But above all, it was Barbara Cartland's overriding belief in the positive power of love to help, heal and improve the quality of life for everyone that made her truly unique.

"We must all open our hearts and allow ourselves to be filled with the power of love"

Barbara Cartland

CHAPTER ONE
1869

"Wilt thou take this man to thy lawful wedded husband – ?"

The Church was hushed as everyone waited for the bride to say, "I will."

When it came, her response was strong and clear. This was the man she loved and she was claiming him with all the fervour of her being, just as he had claimed her.

Lady Elvina Winwood, watching them fondly, was delighted at the sight of her cousin Claudia, who had found perfect happiness. James was a fine young man and this was a splendid wedding.

How beautiful the bride is, Elvina thought, as she offered her left hand to James so that he could place the ring on her finger. Her dress was glorious, all satin and tulle, decorated with lace. The lace veil on her head was a family heirloom.

How beautiful and how gloriously happy! Only true love could bring that kind of joy.

Suddenly the picture of Andrew came into Elvina's mind. Captain Andrew Broadmoor, an ex-army officer who had recently taken up residence on his estate close to hers. He was young, handsome and his passion for horses equalled her own.

When she had left Derbyshire to come to London for her cousin's wedding, Andrew had kissed her hand and told her that she must return soon. There had been a look in his dark eyes that had made her tremble.

Now she seemed to feel the imprint of his lips once more on her hand and remembered the way her heart had beaten faster.

"With this ring, I thee wed – "

The bride and groom were proceeding with the marriage service, becoming truly united.

And then something strange seemed to happen.

Suddenly the bridal couple were no longer Claudia and James, but Elvina and Andrew.

She looked at her cousin in the glorious white gown and veil and saw herself. And the groom, bestowing such an adoring look in his bride, was Andrew.

'It is true,' she thought blissfully. 'I love Andrew and he loves me. When I return home he will ask me to be his wife, and soon we shall be the bridal couple standing before the altar.'

"I now pronounce you man and wife."

The organ swelled and the happy couple turned to leave the Church. Everywhere there were glowing smiles.

The widowed Lady Tranbourn, Elvina's Aunt Alice, was full of triumph at seeing her daughter make such a fine match.

"There," she sighed. "Didn't that go well, Elvina? Elvina?"

Elvina came out of her blissful trance. She felt as though she was bursting with joy at what was happening to her. She knew now that Andrew was the right man for her.

"Yes, aunt," she breathed, "it was a beautiful wedding."

Together they walked out of the Church. It was St. George's, Hanover Square, for, as Aunt Alice had insisted, "everybody who's anybody marries there."

Outside there were carriages waiting to take them back to Tranbourn House in Grosvenor Street, where a huge glittering reception was to take place.

"Well, I hope you are now convinced what an exciting place London can be," Aunt Alice told Elvina as they travelled home. "We don't see you nearly often enough. It is too bad of you to hide yourself away in Derbyshire."

"Dear aunt, it is so kind of you to want me to stay, but my life is in Derbyshire, caring for the estate and Papa's horses."

"You say 'Papa's horses' as though he was still alive. But they are your horses now."

"Yes," Elvina agreed a little sadly. "It is just that I was always so close to Papa, I still think of everything as his."

Her father had died a year ago, leaving her a large estate, a good deal of money and fifty magnificent horses which, after his daughter, were the love of his life.

Lord Winwood had been an Earl and his title plus a certain amount of money had been entailed and had descended to a cousin. But his house and estate and the bulk of his fortune had gone to his beloved daughter, Elvina.

"You still miss him, don't you?" Aunt Alice said gently.

"Yes, terribly. Ever since Mama died four years ago, Papa and I were everything to each other. Now he has gone too."

"And you are living all alone in that great house."

"I am not alone. I have Margaret. We get on very well."

"My dear! A paid companion! And a poor relation at that."

"Aunt, dear!" Elvina protested, laughing. "What a terrible way to describe poor Margaret."

"She *is* a paid companion, isn't she?"

"Well, yes, but – "

"And she *is* a poor relation of your father's family."

"Papa engaged her in the last year of his life so that I should not be all alone when he died. We chose her because she is my own age and we have a lot of interests in common. She too loves riding."

"Oh, well, there is nothing more to be said," Aunt Alice remarked ironically. "If she is a good rider what else is needed?"

"Nothing very much," Elvina admitted with a little laugh.

"I always said that nobody who visited your home would know that your father was an Earl. A horse-breeder perhaps, but not an Earl."

"Well, he *was* a horse-breeder," Elvina conceded. "Everyone in the district came to him for horses because his animals were always the best. I only hope I can keep up his standards. Did you know that if a horse – ?"

"Enough!" Aunt Alice raised her hand imperiously. "From your father I had to endure endless equine talk. From you I cannot and will not. Cease, immediately. When we reach the reception you will doubtless find some young man who will indulge you on the subject."

But young men were more likely to want to talk to Elvina about herself. They would rave about her glossy chestnut curls, her deep green eyes, the hint of a dimple in her chin.

Elvina did not find her own beauty an object of interest and rapidly grew bored with such talk.

Andrew did not pay her extravagant compliments, although she knew that he admired her looks. He talked about horses, for he too was proud of his stable. And sometimes she would turn and find him looking at her in a way that made her heart skip a beat.

"And talking of young men," Aunt Alice resumed, "when are we going to hear of *your* marriage?"

"Aunt, please!" Elvina could not help herself blushing and her aunt saw it.

"So there *is* someone? Why haven't you brought him to the point? All right, you don't have to tell me that I am a nosy busy-body. Marrying people off is one of my pleasures in life. Just see to it that he does not take too long."

To Elvina's relief they had now reached Tranbourn House. The reception swallowed them up and saved her from further inquisition.

After her revelation about Andrew, Elvina found that everything looked different. In a few weeks the glowing bride might be herself. She longed for the party to be over, so that she could be alone to think about Andrew and luxuriate in her love.

"Elvina dear," Aunt Alice called her over, "have you ever met Lady Croften? You both come from the same part of the world."

It turned out that Lady Croften came from Cumberland, but Aunt Alice, a Londoner to her fingertips, somehow felt that anywhere in the northern part of the country must be all the same. Neither of her listeners disillusioned her.

They fell into discussion of the bride.

"I have always been so lucky," Aunt Alice sighed. "Claudia has been a wonderful daughter and I know she will make her husband a superb wife."

"It is because you have brought her up so well," Lady Croften remarked.

"I have done my best, but she is very sensible and she had the most excellent reports from every school she attended."

"Then you really have been lucky," Lady Croften agreed. "I was hearing only yesterday how the Duke of Castleforde is having a great deal of trouble with his sister. He is my neighbour in Cumberland, you know."

"I believe he is a very great man," Aunt Alice commented.

"Oh, yes," Lady Croften said. "Personally he can be charming, but he is a grandee with one of the oldest and most significant titles in the country. Naturally he is proud and wants Lady Violet to be a credit to him and to the family name."

"I have often heard you talking about him," Aunt Alice added.

"He inherited when he was very young and his sister was only a baby. Three years ago his mother died and now he has to look after the girl."

She sighed as she continued,

"Of course for a young man it is a strenuous task which so far, from all I hear, he finds almost impossible."

"But why?" Aunt Alice asked curiously.

6

"Well, the girl just refuses to learn anything. She keeps saying she does not want to be clever. I understand they have employed governess after governess.

"I am sorry for him, because I was very fond of his mother. I met him recently when he was on a visit to London. He asked me if I knew of a governess for his sister and admitted, rather reluctantly, how many governesses she had been through already."

"How many were there?" Elvina asked.

"About half-a-dozen, as far as I can remember. I put him in touch with an excellent woman who was governess to my own girls and she took the job. But she walked out in a month."

There was a small commotion. The bride was ready to retire and don her travelling clothes. Aunt Alice smiled and excused herself.

A lull fell over the party. Nothing could happen now until Claudia came downstairs to depart with her new husband.

At last, to everyone's relief, Claudia appeared and descended the stairs while the guests applauded. She was still carrying her wedding bouquet and she glanced mischievously around before tossing it away.

The bouquet soared high into the air and seemed to hover.

'If I catch it,' Elvina thought, 'I will marry Andrew. If I don't – '

But that was unthinkable.

The bouquet plunged down straight into Elvina's arms.

She could not stop herself giving a big sigh of relief, which everyone saw and roared with laughter.

"Come on, Elvina! Tell us who he is."

But she only smiled and buried her face in the flowers to hide her blushes.

Suddenly she could not bear to stay in London a moment longer. She longed to go home to Derbyshire and see Andrew again. Then she could look into his eyes and know that he felt the same as her.

She joined in the cheers as the happy couple departed for the station. Then she sought out her aunt.

"Dear Aunt Alice, you have been so kind having me to stay and I have really been very happy – "

"But you are missing the young man you were thinking of when you caught the bouquet," her aunt added kindly. "I understand. But you must promise to bring him to see me as soon as possible."

"I will. I promise. And I will write to you just as soon as everything is settled."

That night Elvina packed her things with the help of Aunt Alice's maid.

As she snuggled down in bed, she sighed blissfully thinking over the time she had known Andrew and how those wonderful weeks had all been building up to their marriage.

She remembered her parents' marriage and how wonderful it had been for both of them. Despite all the difficulties they had encountered, they had been the happiest couple she had ever known.

"I loved your mother," her father had told her once, "from the moment I first saw her. We wanted to have a large family but after you were born the doctors said it was impossible for her to have another baby. So you will have to make up for all the other children."

'If I ever marry,' Elvina had thought, 'I want to be as happy as Mama and Papa were together. If things went wrong they laughed and if things went right they shared their happiness, so that it was impossible for anyone or anything to upset or worry them.'

When her mother had died Elvina herself had been a *debutante*, staying with Aunt Alice in London, but she had returned home at once to be with her father.

She had soon recognised that on his own her father had lost the will to live.

Father and daughter had always been close, but in the last four years of his life they had grown even closer. She shared his passion for horses and they loved nothing better than to be together, riding or discussing breeding stock.

But Elvina had known that this could not last. Papa's health was frail and when he said he wanted her to find a companion she guessed that he dreaded leaving her alone.

"You should have a girl of your own age," he said, "someone to share your interests."

A few months ago they had found a very charming girl who was actually a distant relative of the family.

Her name was Margaret and she was delighted to come and live with them. Her parents were dead and she dreaded having to earn a living among strangers.

Elvina liked her, finding that they shared many interests. Margaret too enjoyed riding and loved the music which meant so much to Elvina and her father.

Every evening after dinner, Elvina would go to the piano and play to her father the tunes he had liked ever since he had been young.

Invariably when she had played and sometimes sang the popular tunes, her father would say,

"You ought to be in London. You should have some charming young man telling you that you are the prettiest girl he has ever met."

Elvina laughed.

"I would much rather you say it, Papa," she answered. "You made me go to London to stay with Aunt Alice when I was eighteen, but I felt lonely and somewhat of an outsider."

"Well, I am glad you would rather be here with me," her father said, "I would be very lonely without you."

She was perfectly happy riding every morning with her father, helping him with the new horses which he kept adding to his very large collection.

At the time of his death, she had known that he was happy to rejoin his beloved wife.

Now Elvina was grateful to Papa for having insisted on a companion of her own age, so that she was not completely alone.

And then another figure had come into her life.

She had noticed the young man first because he had been riding a very fine horse. It was only afterwards that she had noticed how handsome he was. And then she realised that he was very good-looking indeed.

He was Captain Andrew Broadmoor, newly out of the Army and owner of the estate nearby.

At their first meeting he had apologised for wandering onto her land and she had smiled and said that all was well.

They had talked about horses and both found them to be more exciting and interesting than people.

"I talk to my horse when I am riding," Elvina had told him. "I feel that he understands everything I say to him."

Andrew laughed.

"I find horses irresistible," he replied. "I bought two more yesterday which I want you to see and tell me if I have secured a bargain."

"I would love to see them. Can I come over this afternoon and bring my friend with me, who is as enthusiastic as I am to make our stable the best in the whole County?"

"You are forgetting that I will be fighting you for that accolade," Andrew retorted.

Elvina shrugged.

"You have a long way to go to catch up with me," she replied. "After all, I inherited over fifty horses when my father died. As you have just come out of the Army, I cannot believe you can have as many as that."

"I have as many as I can afford," Andrew admitted, "and I will be very hurt if you do not admire them."

Elvina and Margaret rode over after luncheon.

It was only two miles to Captain Broadmoor's house which was much larger than she expected. So were his stables.

But his horses were a disappointment – few in number, and none of them matched up to the excellent stallion Elvina had seen him riding. But she was far too polite to say so.

She found that it was rather charming to have a young man as a neighbour. When her father had been alive his friends in the country had been his own age.

"We are two young people," she had once said to Margaret, "amongst those who are double our age."

11

"But at least we have the Captain to cheer us up," Margaret reminded her.

He must have felt the same, because he was continually popping in to see them and consulting Elvina about the horses he was determined to buy.

"I have a long way to go before my stables equal yours," he admitted, "but I find it impossible to say no when I am offered a bargain."

"You must not spend what you cannot afford," Elvina advised him. "Don't be in so much of a hurry. Remember that horses not only cost money but eat money, as my father used to say."

She spoke cautiously because she had come to understand that Andrew was not well-off in comparison to herself.

"I heard of an excellent new horse today," he had said recently, "and I think I should buy it before it's offered to you because I know you will take it."

"Are you depriving me of something I ought to acquire?" she asked.

"No, I am only protecting you from having too much," Andrew answered. "Your stables are bulging and mine, as you have pointed out, are extremely empty."

"You will have to look after my horses next week," she told him, "as I have to go to my cousin Claudia's wedding in London. I will be away for at least a week."

"I promise I will exercise your horses and keep an eye on them," Andrew had said. "Are you taking Margaret with you?"

Elvina shook her head.

"No," she replied. "They have only asked me."

"Then I will look after Margaret too," he offered. "But hurry back."

The week before she left, she rode every morning with Andrew. He was a better rider than Margaret and they both rode so fast that it was a joy for them and the horses they rode.

On the day that she left he had pressed her hand and said,

"I will miss you dreadfully."

"I feel guilty about going," she told him. "But I will feel less guilty knowing that you are here."

"I always want to be here," he told her.

There was an expression in his eyes which Elvina had not seen before.

She found herself thinking about him on her way to London.

She knew, although she had not thought about it earlier, that he meant so much to her and things might be very different if he was not there.

'Can I be falling in love with him?' she asked herself repeatedly.

Then almost as if she had suddenly woken up, she was sure that he was in love with her.

There were comments he had made which were of no particular importance. But now, when she remembered them, it seemed to her that the words held a new significance.

She was pondering these thoughts for the whole week she was in London attending parties, meeting other young men and finding them dull. Now she knew that they were dull because none of them was Andrew.

Next day she left her aunt's house immediately after breakfast. The carriage took her to the railway station and she boarded the train for Derby. From there she changed onto a small local line that dropped her half a mile from her home.

A passing farmer offered her a lift on his cart. She left her luggage at the station, telling the station master that someone would come to collect it, and she spent the rest of the journey enjoying the thought of Margaret's face when she walked in unexpectedly.

Then she would take her best horse from the stable and gallop over to see Andrew. Picturing their joyous reunion made her shiver with pleasurable anticipation.

She walked the last few hundred yards, approaching the house from the back and letting herself in by the kitchen door.

There was no one in the kitchen and she slipped quietly into the hall.

And at once she saw Andrew's hat and riding whip on one of the chairs.

'He is here,' she thought. 'He must have come to ask Margaret if she had heard any news from me.'

She hurried down the passage which led to the room which her father had used as his smoking room. She reached the door and was just about to open it when she heard a man's voice, and knew that Andrew was inside and was talking to someone.

There was a curtain over the door which protected those in the room from draughts in the winter.

Without really thinking what she was doing, Elvina pushed open the door not making a sound.

Then she heard Andrew's voice saying,

"I love you, I love you, you know I do. But there is no possible chance of my holding my estate together unless I ask Elvina to marry me."

There was silence for a moment.

Then Elvina heard Margaret say,

"How can you do that when we love each other? love you, Andrew, with all my heart. But, despite what you say, I cannot really believe that you love me."

"I *do* love you," Andrew answered, "with all my heart and soul. But I need money. There has been a terrible crash on the Stock Market and I find myself practically penniless."

"Oh, it cannot be true," Margaret said with a sob.

"It is true," Andrew replied. "I have tried to avoid it and I have tried to pretend it isn't happening, but it *has* happened. I have to sell all my horses, my house and everything I possess and even then I will still be in debt."

"I don't understand," Margaret sighed in a whisper.

"I have to find at least two thousand pounds to keep what I possess," Andrew added sombrely. Even then I will find it very difficult to keep my head above water."

"So there is nothing you can do but marry Elvina," Margaret sobbed. "But does she love you?"

"I think so," Andrew replied, "and I am very fond of her. But you are the one I love and have done from the first moment I saw you."

"How can I live without you?" Margaret asked passionately.

"Or I without you," Andrew answered. "But I have no choice, even though I feel I will die without you."

"You will break my heart," Margaret wept. "I will never love anyone but you. Is there any way we can be together?"

"How can I ask you to live in poverty, watching you dying in misery? Then I would only want to die myself."

"You must do what you think is right," Margaret said forlornly.

"My precious, my darling, I knew you would understand," Andrew told her. "Although, God knows, I will regret it every day of my life."

"She will be home any day soon," Margaret said. "And then I suppose – ?"

"Yes, I dare not leave it any longer. I must propose at once and the sooner we marry the better. Heaven knows how I shall live with her. Perhaps if I pretend she's you – " He broke off with a groan.

"I must go away," Margaret murmured.

"Yes," he said, "for I must try to be faithful to Elvina, although it breaks my heart. Oh, my darling, my darling, kiss me, *kiss me!*"

There was a long silence and Elvina guessed that they were in each other's arms, locked in a passionate embrace.

Slowly she turned away from the door.

Walking on tiptoe she crossed the hall and climbed up the stairs to her bedroom.

When she reached it she stood looking at a portrait of her father which hung near her bed.

Elvina stood gazing at it for a long time before she asked,

"What am I to do, Papa? *Tell me what I am to do.*"

CHAPTER TWO

In the first hideous shock of discovering that the man she loved had turned away from her and loved another, Elvina had frozen. Then her only thought had been to escape before they discovered her.

But now she had gone well away from them, all the bitterness and anguish of her situation welled up and a violent sob shook her.

She wanted to cry aloud to Heaven that she had been betrayed. Margaret had come into her house and stolen the man she loved in a devious and underhand way.

But she did not cry to Heaven. She leaned against the wall while tears poured down her face. She loved Andrew and now she had learned in the most brutal way that he did not love her.

Worse, he was a deceitful schemer, coldly and cynically planning to swear his love to her so that he could get his hands on her money.

He planned to marry her for money and spend their life together pretending that she was Margaret.

She felt as though her heart would break.

After a while she forced herself to be calm. At all costs she must not let herself be found in the house. But where could she turn for help?

She returned to her father's portrait, feeling that somehow and somewhere he knew what was happening to her.

'Help me! *Help me!*' she cried from her heart.

Then she knew the answer, just as though he had spoken to her.

She must go away. Not just out of the house for a while, but far away for a long time.

She must not let them realise that she had discovered what had happened.

She shivered at the picture of herself that Andrew had presented to her – a little rich girl, using her wealth to snare a man whose heart belonged to another woman.

Was she really that vulgar a creature?

No, she decided. She would prove them wrong. Somehow she would make it possible for Andrew and Margaret to marry each other. Only then would she be truly free of them and be able to put this terrible day behind her.

'But how can I do that?' she asked herself.

Then, again as though her father had inspired her, she knew the answer.

Drying her eyes, she hurried across the room to a desk where she wrote her letters. Sitting down, she wrote out a banker's draft in the name of Andrew Broadmoor.

She hesitated before she wrote, 'two thousand pounds.'

Then she signed it, put it into an envelope and addressed it to Andrew.

Next, she returned to the portrait of her father, and pleaded,

'Now what shall I do, Papa? Where shall I go? cannot stay here and argue about what has happened.'

She waited almost as if she would hear an answer from her father. But there was only a silence that seemed to ring in her ears.

When he received the cheque, Andrew would press her to marry him. How could any man accept such an enormous gift from a woman without in some way paying for it?

She felt suddenly as if she was alone in a place she did not know and that she was in danger.

'I am frightened,' she whispered. 'Help me, Papa, please help me. I am afraid that Andrew will argue with me and force me to take the money back. I still love him. cannot help it. If he wants me to marry him, I might weaken and agree. And I *must* not. We could never be happy.

'But where can I go? Not back to London. They will wonder why I have returned so soon.'

Then suddenly she heard a voice in her head – Lady Croften, at the wedding reception, saying,

'The Duke of Castleforde is having a great deal of trouble with his sister – he inherited when he was very young – since her mother died the girl just refuses to learn anything. She is horse mad and spends her life in the stables – they have had governess after governess.'

This was the answer to her prayer. The Duke lived in Cumberland and no one would think of looking for her there. Andrew would believe she was still with her relations in London.

'I must leave at once,' she told herself. 'If the Duke has no use for me, I am sure I will be able to find something else to do.'

Leaving the letter to Andrew on her desk, she put the chequebook into her bag, turned and ran out of the room and down the back stairs.

She found her way through the passages which led to the scullery. The back door was open and she slipped through it, heading back the way she had come.

There was no cart to take her, so she set herself to walk the distance.

Her heart ached and she wept as she trudged on, but she had set her course and would not be turned aside from it now.

She reached the little station at last, thankful that she had left her luggage there. In answer to her question the porter told her that there was a train back to Derby in ten minutes. And from Derby there was a connection to Arnside in Cumberland.

He carried her bags over to the far platform for her and soon she was on her way back to Derby. There she had only a short wait. The train to Arnside was on time and at last she was able to sink back into her seat and think clearly about what had happened.

She loved Andrew but he did not love her. Worse still, he was prepared to marry her cynically for her money.

How easy she had made it for him by going to London. He must have ridden over every day to see Margaret and their love had flourished.

'I will not think about it,' she told herself firmly. 'I just hope the Duke will employ me. If he doesn't, I can always go travelling, but a post as a governess will hide me better because nobody would ever think of it.'

Now it was time to be practical. It would be early evening before she reached Arnside and too late to go to the Duke's estate.

'I will stay the night at a hotel,' she thought. 'There is probably one close to the station. And I will tell them I am a married woman. A single girl alone attracts too much attention.'

She remembered that her initials, E.W., were on some of her suitcases. So she needed a name that fitted them.

'I will be Mrs. Winters. It will be easy to remember, because now it is *winter* in my heart.'

She reflected that she was losing not only the man she loved, but also the girl who had been a wonderful companion and friend, someone who had been almost as dear to her as a sister.

At the *Railway Hotel* she booked a room without any trouble in the name of Mrs. Winters. She ate an excellent dinner and in the hall she found a book about the locality, which she took up to bed.

As she had hoped, there was a chapter about Castleforde Castle, which was about twenty miles away.

'The house was started by the first Duke of Castleforde in the twelfth century and has been added to by subsequent Dukes over the generations. Parts of the original castle can still be seen in the centre block, but there is now a Tudor wing, a Jacobean wing and a Georgian wing.'

It seemed to be a huge estate with a mansion full of art works. Elvina was intrigued.

At last she put out the light and settled down in bed.

She had the strongest feeling that her father was looking over her and was approving of all she was doing.

'I am running away, Papa,' she murmured. 'But what else could I have done? Somehow I know you are helping me.

'Perhaps one day, if God is kind, and you, darling Papa, are guiding me from Heaven, I will find a man who will love me for myself and not because you left me money.

'He will love me because I am an equal part of his heart and soul.'

She fell asleep.

*

Next morning she hired a cab to take her to Castleforde Castle.

The journey lay through some of the loveliest countryside she had ever seen, and she remembered that this part of England was known as the Lake District because of the number of large and beautiful lakes and the magnificent scenery that surrounded them.

Suddenly, just ahead, she saw high double wrought iron gates. Each side bore a huge crest that Elvina recognised as the coat of arms of the Dukes of Castleforde. She had seen it in the book last night.

On one side of the gates was the porter's lodge, out of which a man emerged and approached the carriage.

"I am Mrs. Winters," Elvina said through the window. "I am here to see the Duke about a position as governess."

She thought the porter muttered, "another one?" before turning away and pulling open the gates for the cab to pass through.

There was still a mile to go before the castle came into view. Then it was in front of her. The original building could easily be seen in the centre with its turrets and battlements. And there on the largest turret was a flagpole with a flag flying bravely.

Elvina gave a sigh of relief. At least the Duke was at home.

As the cab drew up outside the front door, Elvina climbed out and said to the driver,

"You had better wait here, please."

Boldly she knocked on the door and after a moment it was opened by the butler.

"I would like to see His Grace," Elvina stated. "I understand he is looking for a governess."

"Oh, yes, ma'am," the butler replied, wooden-faced. "His Grace is always looking for a governess. I will take you to him."

He started to walk along the passage in front of her with Elvina following. Glancing around her, she saw that the building was magnificent inside as well. It had been well maintained over the centuries and she could sense the history that permeated the walls.

After what Elvina had read the night before, she felt she had a good idea of that history.

The name of Castleforde had always been prominent in England. In whatever age, whatever reign, there had always been a Castleforde beside the monarch, exercising influence, either openly or secretly.

Starting as Barons they had finished as Dukes. Their daughters had married great titles, sometimes even minor royalty.

Their portraits lined the walls, stern-faced matrons covered in jewels, glamorous men, covered in even more jewels. Their fingers lingered on the ruby-studded hilts of their daggers. Their eyes gleamed with ambition.

"What name shall I tell His Grace?" the butler asked.

"Mrs. Winters."

He was leading her to the rear of the castle. Suddenly he stopped before a huge oak panelled door, pushed it open and announced,

"A Mrs. Winters to see you, Your Grace."

She moved past him and found herself in an impressive library. Row upon row of shelves soared up to the ceiling, so that ladders had to be used to reach the top shelves.

At first Elvina thought the room was empty and turned to the butler in dismay. But he had withdrawn and the door was closing behind him.

Baffled, she looked around, until a voice from above her said,

"I am up here."

She saw him then, sitting up high on a ladder, looking down at her.

He was in his thirties, with a face that would have been exceedingly handsome but for his air of sternness and gravity.

There was no doubt that he was a Castleforde. He boasted the family features, lean and fine, and the family eyes that were dark and brilliant.

Lady Croften had said that he was a proud man and Elvina could see that it was true. He was neither lofty nor imperious, but even at this angle he had the indefinable air of a man who had lived at the top of the aristocratic tree since birth, and could imagine no other place for himself.

"You have come to see me?" he asked.

"My name is Mrs. Winters," Elvina began.

"So my butler said."

"It is very difficult while you are up there," she said. "I am getting a crick in my neck."

"I'm sorry."

He descended the ladder, jumping the last few steps. Now she could see that he was very tall, over six feet.

"Here I am," he said. "But I must tell you, Mrs. Winters, that it is not my custom to see people without an appointment."

His voice was rich and pleasant but serious and he was regarding her as though uncertain of what to make of her.

It did not make for an auspicious beginning.

"I appreciate that this may look a little odd," she answered cautiously, "but I was told by some friends that you are looking for a governess for your sister. They suggested that I should call on you when I was in this part of the country.

"Of course I should have notified you first, but my decision was made suddenly."

"Are you a governess?"

"I know a great deal about training young women who are leaving school."

The Duke stared at her as if, for some reason, he found this hard to believe. Then he said,

"Please sit down and I can tell you exactly what I require. I hope, although it may be impossible, that you will succeed where, as you have doubtless been told, other women have failed."

"I have been told that they just walk out," Elvina said. "Although how anyone can bear to leave this lovely place amazes me."

For the first time he smiled.

"It *is* lovely, isn't it?" he said. "I think it is the most wonderful place on earth. I love its history, and the knowledge that my family have played an important role in this country for centuries.

"If only my sister felt the same. She just wants to get out of the schoolroom as fast as possible and start enjoying herself as a *debutante*. I try to tell her that no young man will be interested in a girl who has learned nothing in her life."

"Nothing at all?" Elvina asked, surprised.

"Well, something, obviously. Even Violet hasn't been through school and governesses without learning something. I know she's intelligent. She learned to read when she was only four."

"Doesn't she read now?"

"Oh, yes. Periodicals called *The Modern Young Lady* and *The Debutante's Friend,* full of fashion plates and foolish stories."

"I read those when I was her age. They do no harm, and sometimes a lot of good."

"Good?" he echoed, startled.

"They reinforce good principles," Elvina responded, assuming the serious demeanour that she felt would impress him most. The stories are always extremely moral, as I expect you have noticed."

"I?" His outrage was so vehement that she almost laughed. "I – read such things?"

"But if you haven't read them, how do you know they are foolish?" Elvina questioned him demurely.

Suddenly and with perfect timing, a memory from the book she had read the previous evening, came into her mind.

"Did not your illustrious ancestor, the second Duke, advise King James I, '*Let no man speak of that which lies hidden from his eyes.*'?"

Then was an astonished silence. Then the Duke's lips twitched.

"It was the third Duke, actually," he stated quietly.

"The third, of course. How could I have forgotten that?"

Again there was a gleam of humour in his eyes, suggesting that there was more to this man than aristocratic pride.

"You are well informed, Mrs. Winters," he said. "I compliment you. Tell me, did you study my family's history before you came here?"

She hesitated and then decided that the strict truth would serve her best.

"I did, for precisely one hour last night. My hotel had a book on the locality and I made a point of reading the chapter about the Dukes of Castleforde. What you have just heard me recite is the beginning and end of my knowledge."

"Then I compliment you again for your honesty and your shrewdness. Whatever else you are, you are no fool."

"And what else do you think I might be?" she asked, daringly.

He seemed taken by surprise.

"That is something that I would not undertake to speculate about," he answered slowly. "Not just yet. Tell me something about yourself. Is there a Mr. Winters?"

"No longer."

"Then you are a widow and he left you in straightened circumstances, since you have to earn your living."

"Not precisely. I have an income large enough to live comfortably, but I detest idleness and would rather be useful. I am extremely well educated and I dislike waste. I speak French and Italian. I can dance, sing and ride."

Suddenly he shot out a question.

"Tell me, who is the Prime Minister?"

"Mr. Gladstone, of course," Elvina replied at once. "He won the general election last year."

"So you know something about what is going on in the country. That's a relief. It might be happening on the other side of the moon for all that Violet knows or cares."

"Well, that should be remedied naturally," Elvina agreed. "But when she is dancing around a ballroom in the arms of some eligible young man, he will want to be talking about something other than Mr. Gladstone. After all, do you discuss elections with young ladies when you are dancing with them?"

He grinned. "A good point, madam. I will remember that the next time I am dancing with a beautiful young lady. But Violet is the daughter of a Duke. She will move in the first circles, which means not just that she will meet other aristocrats, but gentlemen who are going into politics.

"Her husband will probably sit in the House of Lords. If not, he may be elected to the Commons, even become Prime Minister. She must be sufficiently well-informed to be a credit to those who raised her."

"How old is Violet?"

"She is almost seventeen," the Duke replied, "so in a year she will be a *debutante*. I naturally want her to be a great success."

"I find it hard to understand how she could fail to appreciate this castle," Elvina commented. "Even the little I have seen is a history lesson in itself."

"I am very sure that she does not see it like that," the Duke sighed.

"I expect it's because one never appreciates what one has always known since birth," Elvina replied. "Most of us long for what we have never seen, more than what we can see."

The Duke stared at her.

She looked back at him, thinking how very handsome he was, especially when he gave one of his rare smiles.

"Yes, I suppose that is true," he agreed. "I am beginning to feel that you could be the one person who might help me. I am being honest, telling you how hopeless the whole situation feels.

"If you are brave enough to try what has been impossible for so many other women, I can only tell you how grateful I would be. But I do not want you to be deceived into thinking such a task will be easy."

"Of course I realise the problems," Elvina told him. "But I enjoy a challenge."

"Do you really think you have a chance?" the Duke asked. "You are still very young."

"I am older than I look," Elvina responded quickly. "I think I can cope with most eventualities. But I would like to know why Violet has this attitude. Has she always been this way?"

"No, only since she was twelve. That was when my mother died. An aunt came to stay with us and on her advice I sent Violet to a school in London.

29

"It was a failure from the very beginning. She hated school, perhaps because she was missing her mother. She ran away, and I hadn't the heart to send her back when she was so unhappy. My aunt was furious and stormed out. thought Violet and I could manage together with the help of a governess."

The Duke paused for breath and Elvina enquired,

"But that plan failed too?"

"Completely and absolutely," the Duke replied. "I took her on a visit to London. We went to the theatre several times. I thought she would enjoy it."

"And didn't she?"

"Too much," he groaned. "Her latest notion is to be an actress. Can you imagine anything so absurd? That my sister, a Castleforde, should want to take up such a vulgar, tawdry way of life, where the women are little better than – forgive me, I should not speak of such things."

"Never fear, I think I am unshockable," Elvina told him. "And it's best for me to know what I will have to contend with. Depend on it, she sees only the glamorous and romantic side of the theatre. She has no idea that the life of an actress leaves much to be desired."

"And I do not want her to find out," the Duke said firmly. "I have tried explaining to her that it's impossible – "

"And only made it sound more attractive," Elvina observed.

"I suppose so," he sighed. "Now we live in a permanent state of armed truce. She flees the house to spend her days riding."

Elvina did not say so but she thought that this was a point in Violet's favour.

Aloud she said,

"Allow me to meet your sister, please"

"I will take you up to her."

Then a thought seemed to strike him.

"Wait – let me talk to her first. If I spring you on her it may simply make her more difficult. Stay here and I will be back in a moment."

Elvina would have protested but he was gone before she could speak. This was not what she had wanted at all.

Left alone she looked around the library, marvelling at its extent. How she would love to explore all those books, she thought.

She mounted a few steps on one of the ladders. Then a few steps more, her excitement growing with every moment. She reached out and pulled a volume from one of the shelves, making herself comfortable on the ladder so that she could read.

At first she scarcely heard the clatter on the terrace outside. Then the French windows were thrown open and a young girl stormed into the room.

"They say you've brought another governess here," she cried. "But I've told you I won't have it. Why won't you ever listen to me? I won't have a governess, I won't, I – where are you?"

In her fury she had not, at first, noticed that she was alone. Now she came to a halt and glared around her.

"Where are you?" she demanded.

"I am up here," Elvina declared.

CHAPTER THREE

Startled, the girl looked up quickly and her eyes met Elvina's gazing down at her.

"Is it you?" she demanded. "Are you the new governess, because if so, I won't have you. Go away. I don't want you."

Elvina climbed down the ladder and faced her. The girl glared back. She was small and pretty with large glittering blue eyes and an air of fury. In fact, she resembled nothing so much as a dainty, infuriated wasp.

"I don't want you," she repeated.

"It seems that nobody wants me," Elvina replied.

"What are you saying?"

Elvina thought quickly.

"I am saying that I need your help," she confided in a low voice. "Nobody else must know what I am about to tell you."

The girl stared at her in astonishment.

"My help?" she exclaimed.

"Please, please help me," Elvina pleaded. "If you can't, then I will have to leave and – " she shuddered, "I am afraid of doing that."

Violet's eyes widened.

"Tell me why you are afraid," she asked.

She was looking at Elvina in a fierce manner which might have frightened anyone else away. But there was curiosity in her eyes too.

"And why have you come here?"

"I have come here to hide," she confessed, "because some terrible things have happened to me. I couldn't think of anywhere to stay, but I heard you wanted a governess, so I pretended to be one so that I could hide here."

The girl's eyes widened.

"You are not a governess?" she exclaimed.

"No, of course not," Elvina replied. "I had a governess myself and I know what horrors they can be."

Violet regarded her curiously, as though not sure what to make of someone who talked like this.

"Does my brother know how you feel?" she asked at last.

"Certainly not," Elvina said, "and please promise me on everything you hold sacred that you will keep my secret."

"As long as you are *not* a governess."

"Of course not. I have never taught anybody anything in my life," Elvina declared with perfect truth. "That is why this is the safest place for me to hide, because nobody who knows me will think for a moment that I am pretending to be a governess. Also I have given your brother a false name."

Violet's eyes gleamed at this hint of conspiracy. She bent forward to be a little nearer to Elvina.

"What name?" she asked.

"I have told him that I am Mrs. Winters."

"But you're not?"

"I am not."

"Then what is your real name?" Violet whispered.

"If I told you that there would be no point in giving a false one," she replied.

"What are you hiding from?" she asked.

Elvina took a shuddering breath.

"From the man I love," she said simply.

"Tell me all about it," Violet gasped.

"When my father died he left me a lot of money. I expect if I told you his name, your brother would have heard of him."

"But what happened?" Violet quizzed her in an agony of anticipation.

"I visited London to attend my cousin's wedding, but I came home early to be with the man I loved. Nobody saw me arrive and that was how I overheard this man talking to my companion, telling her that he loved her."

"Her? Not you?"

"Not me. But he was planning to marry me for my money. He actually said that. But then he said again that he loved her as he had never loved anyone else."

Elvina's voice faltered on the last words.

Aghast, Violet exclaimed, "You *heard* him say that!"

"Yes, I heard it all," Elvina replied.

"Has he told you that he loved you?"

"In a roundabout way. And I had only just realised how much I loved him. I travelled home, full of excitement, longing to see him."

"Did he actually ask you to marry him?"

"No, but he hinted at it and I was sure that I wanted to say yes.

"I promised my mother before she died that unless I fell in love with both my heart and my soul, I would not marry anyone. She had been so happy with my father that she was afraid lest I should not know the same happiness. I was so sure that I had found it."

Elvina's voice seemed to break and after a moment Violet said,

"I am so sorry for you. It must have been a terrible shock."

"I didn't have the slightest idea that he found my companion attractive in that sort of way. He was always very polite to her, but it seems that this was there between them all the time."

"What did you do?"

"I knew that I couldn't stay at home waiting for him to ask me to marry him for my money. I had to leave at once, before they knew that I had heard them."

"But why did you have to run away?"

"Because I couldn't face him lying to me," Elvina answered, "and saying that he loved me when all the time he loved another woman. I thought that would be degrading and horrible and I could not bear it."

"But why couldn't you take your revenge on them?" Violet wanted to know. "You could have stormed in and berated them for betraying you. Then you could have dismissed your companion and ordered the man never to darken your doors again."

"That is what you would have done, is it?" Elvina asked with a faint smile.

"Of course. If any man betrayed me I would make him suffer for it," Violet declared melodramatically.

"One day you may discover that it isn't as simple as that. If you love someone you don't want to hurt him, whatever he has done. And it was hardly my companion's fault that she fell in love."

"You mean you don't hate them?" Violet asked.

Elvina shook her head and for a moment her eyes became misty.

"No," she whispered. "I don't hate them."

"But how did you manage to come here?"

"When I was in London I heard someone saying that your brother, the Duke, was desperately trying to find a governess for you since you did not wish to go to school."

Violet chuckled suddenly.

"You mean since I was such a little horror, don't you?"

"They may have said something like that," Elvina told her cautiously and Violet chuckled again.

But then she grew serious suddenly, as though something had occurred to her.

"Didn't you do anything about him?" she asked. "Write him a letter so full of scorn that it burned the page, maybe?"

"I left him a cheque for two thousand pounds," Elvina admitted.

"You *rewarded* him for – ?"

"I thought it might prevent him trying to find me, but perhaps I miscalculated and he will feel more obliged to offer for me now."

"Miscalculated?" Violet exclaimed wildly. "You have windmills in your head, that's why you are in such a mess. Goodness, what a muddle!"

"I suppose I am always in a muddle in one way or another," Elvina replied. "But now I am begging you, on my knees if necessary, to let me stay here and hide."

"Of course," Violet said slowly. "You will be much safer here. I will tell David that I have given in, but very reluctantly."

"You must certainly be reluctant," Elvina agreed. "Otherwise he might suspect that I am not a real governess and then he will find somebody else."

"Oh, no, I don't want anyone but you," Violet said quickly.

"We will have to make it look convincing," Elvina added, "but that won't be hard. After all, we will enjoy ourselves talking about things which are really interesting.

"We'll go riding, so that we can't be overheard and the horses certainly won't tell your brother we talked in English rather than in French, or did not say enough about the Holy Lands."

The girl laughed as if she could not help it.

"Are you really saying," she asked, "that we will have pretend lessons?"

"Yes and no. In a sense they will be real lessons. You can gain all sorts of knowledge by admiring the flowers in the garden, by counting the stars in the sky and by whispering under the moon."

"That's the most sensible thing I have ever heard. Of course one learns many things, although they may not be in the school books."

"I will certainly be learning something from *you*," Elvina said, "and hopefully you will be learning something from *me*.

"Knowledge comes in many ways. Sometimes you listen to spoken words, sometimes you can see it in the sky and sometimes you hear it in the wind.

"Perhaps it is clearest when one is praying and, in some extraordinary way, God manages to help you. Just as He sent me here to you when I was desperate."

Violet stared at her, amazed. Then she said,

"You are different from anyone I have ever met. Everything you say is fascinating. We will teach each other. Fancy that!"

She gave a sudden crow of laughter.

"How astonished David will be to see me accept you without a fuss. Oh, I *do* like this plan."

"I was so sure you would reject me that I told the cab driver to wait, just in case I had to return with him. Goodness! He must still be there. I should go and tell him I am staying."

"I'll come with you," Violet offered.

Together they hurried out of the room, down the long passages and into the hall. The doorman saw them coming and pulled the front door open for them.

Later he confided to the butler,

"When I saw the way the two young ladies were running, I thought it was the usual and Lady Violet was throwing the new governess out. But blow me, if they didn't have the cab unloaded."

He was not the only one amazed. The Duke, appearing on the scene a moment later was astonished by the sight that met his eyes.

"Violet, I have been looking everywhere for you. have a new governess for you, and I want you to promise me that you will be very polite and – where are the footmen carrying those cases?"

"Upstairs, brother dear. I have ordered them to be put in the room next to mine. Then Mrs. Winters can keep a really strict eye on me."

The Duke regarded her cautiously.

"What – are you saying?"

"I am saying that since you are determined to force a governess on me to crush my spirit – "

"Violet, my dear girl – "

But Violet was well into the part now and was not going to be sidetracked.

"I have no choice but to submit to your tyrannical demands," she declaimed, her voice on the verge of a sob.

"My what?"

"I have yielded. I will be a dutiful sister, however much it goes against the grain. I say no more."

"I went to look for you," the Duke said, "meaning to bring you down to meet Mrs. Winters. Evidently the two of you have already met."

"Mrs. Winters and I have introduced ourselves," Violet confirmed with lofty dignity.

"And had a useful discussion?"

"Lady Violet and I have discussed many subjects," Elvina remarked, with a firm look at Violet who had moved behind her brother and looked as though her mirth was threatening to overcome her.

Elvina added,

"I believe we now understand each other."

"And do you think you can keep her in order?"

"I didn't exactly say that," Elvina observed wryly.

"Well, you and I will discuss terms later."

"It's only for a month," Violet said, belatedly remembering her lines. "If it doesn't work out, I will send her away."

"You most certainly will not!" her harassed brother growled.

"I will, I will!"

"That's quite enough!" Elvina intervened sternly. "I think we should go upstairs now."

She inclined her head towards the Duke.

"Your Grace may safely leave the problem to me."

"Thank you," he said with relief.

Elvina followed Violet up to the corridor where her room was situated. The room next door was already being prepared by a flurry of maids.

"We will go next door to my room, until yours is ready," Violet suggested, leading the way.

As soon as Violet's door was closed behind them Elvina exclaimed,

"You little wretch. What do you think you are doing?"

"Having fun," Violet gurgled. "Did you see my brother's face?"

"Yes, I did, and the poor man does not know what to think."

"Oh, goody! I'm going to enjoy this."

"Don't go too far or you will arouse his suspicions," Elvina said firmly.

Then inspiration came to her and she added,

"Speak the speech, I pray you – trippingly on the tongue."

"What's that?" Violet asked, frowning.

"That is Hamlet's advice to the players. He gives a whole list of instructions about good acting. I would have thought an actress would have known that."

Now she had really caught Violet's attention. The girl became very still.

"How did you know that I am an actress."

"Your brother told me."

"You mean he said I had this outrageous idea, quite unworthy of a Ducal family – "

"He may have said something of the kind, I didn't listen very closely. I am far more interested in your views."

"But David won't let me be an actress."

"What has it to do with your brother? An actress is made *in here.*" Elvina pointed to her heart. "If you are an actress in your heart, all the brothers in the world cannot change that."

Violet beamed.

"Yes, of course," she agreed ecstatically.

"Have you read the advice to the players?"

Violet shrugged.

"I may have done once at school."

"You should read it again. You will find several useful pointers for when you start your career."

"You mean as an actress?"

"Why not?" Elvina asked crossing her fingers and praying that Heaven would forgive her.

"But David won't let me and he is my guardian."

"Well you are not always going to be underage, are you? Once you turn twenty-one you can do as you please."

"But that's years away."

"It will give you time to practise different parts. You need experience of life as well as experience on the stage."

"David expects me to make a suitable marriage."

"I am sure he would never actually force you. So you will be courted by young men, who will worship you. You will treat them with lofty disdain, secure in the knowledge that inwardly you belong to your art."

"Oh, *yes*," Violet breathed. "That's what I will do."

41

There was a knock at the door. Opening it, Elvina saw a footman, who handed her a note.

"From His Grace, madam," he said, bowing.

The note was brief and to the point.

'Mrs. Winters, I would be obliged if you and Violet would dine with me this evening. Please try to ensure that Violet looks like a lady and not a tomboy.

Castleforde

"Ahah!" Violet exclaimed, peering over Elvina's shoulder. She addressed the footman. "How like him to write like that! Please inform His Grace that Mrs. Winters and Lady Violet will be pleased to join him."

"Yes, my Lady."

The footman bowed himself away.

"I have had an idea," Elvina said. "It is something which will amuse you and will certainly surprise your brother."

"Do tell me," Violet begged.

"Amongst my clothes, I have a very smart dress which I bought in Paris," Elvina said. "I suggest you put it on for dinner and I'll do your hair fashionably. I expect you have plenty of jewellery of your own and you will appear for dinner as the perfect *debutante* in waiting."

Violet stared at her.

"If I do that my brother will faint with surprise," she said.

"Splendid. It will do him good to receive a shock."

"He will think he's dreaming. I have never dressed up since I came home from my last school. Whenever I have taken a meal with my brother I have usually had an argument with him during the first course, then we don't speak for the rest of the meal."

"I guessed it was something like that," smiled Elvina.

"Let us see if your room is ready," Violet suggested.

Since Elvina's room adjoined Violet's it offered the same level of luxury. It was beautifully furnished containing a large, four-poster bed with a canopy and rich brocade curtains.

She walked to the window and saw that the sun was sinking in the sky, casting a golden glow over the view of the park. She had come to a special and beautiful place and she realised that in many ways she was fortunate.

If only she could ignore the ache in her heart that said it should all have been so different.

But when she turned back into the room she was smiling. Nobody must guess at her secret grief.

"Let me show you the dress I want you to wear," she proposed brightly.

She went to the wardrobe as she spoke and took out a dress made of chiffon decorated with flowers. The flowers were picked out in diamante so that the dress glittered as it moved.

Violet stared at it in astonishment.

"Oh, it is so beautiful," she said. "I cannot wait to wear it. What will you wear?"

"I will show you later. First I need to wash off the dust from my journey."

Maids came in dragging a hip bath, which they filled with hot water. Elvina soaked long and luxuriously until it was time to climb out and dress.

Now she was glad that she had fled her home with the luggage she had brought from London, otherwise she would not have brought anything suitable for dining with the Duke.

The evening dress she chose was demure, but even so, it was lower in the bosom than would normally be considered suitable for a governess.

Violet came in with her maid, who helped Elvina put the chiffon dress on her and then started on her hair.

Under Elvina's instructions she lifted Violet's fair hair onto the top of her head, where Elvina placed some artificial flowers. They too were covered with diamante so that Violet looked as if she was wearing a tiara.

"You look lovely," Elvina enthused. "I cannot wait to see your brother's face."

"I think he will be very surprised, as I have often refused to dress up for dinner," Violet admitted. "Sometimes I haven't even changed, which has annoyed him, because he always changes for dinner."

She sighed before adding,

"He sits at the top of the table where our father used to sit. Just like a patriarch."

"And the poor man is too young to be a patriarch."

"Poor man?" Violet echoed. "David isn't a poor man. He is a tyrant."

"I do not think it can have been very easy for him, inheriting his title so young. You might spare a little sympathy for him."

She stood back and regarded Violet.

"Now, you look perfect. Let me go down first and prepare your entrance."

She walked downstairs quickly and the butler guided her to the dining room.

"Don't announce me," she whispered. "I will just slip in."

She entered so quietly that the Duke did not at first notice her. He was standing by the French windows, looking out into the grounds.

He was elegantly dressed in white tie and tails, just as though the Queen was coming to dine. There was no doubt that this was a great aristocrat who maintained formal standards, even in the privacy of his own home.

Elvina advanced into the room at the same moment that the Duke turned and saw her. She saw the surprise in his eyes as her elegant attire.

This was not what was expected of a governess and she briefly wondered if he thought she was being presumptuous. But then he smiled.

"Mrs. Winters. Is Violet with you or has she run away?"

"All is well, I promise you, Your Grace. Violet will be down in a moment. I do not know why you should expect the worst."

"Probably because the worst has happened so often."

"But perhaps you make it happen by expecting it," she suggested gently.

"I am not sure that I understand that."

"Violet knows that you think badly of her – "

"But I – that is entirely untrue. I do not think badly of her, I merely – "

"Merely show that she disappoints you," Elvina finished.

"Is it wrong for me to want her to live up to her position?"

"Well, yes, it might be. Your Grace, will you think me very impudent if I suggest that you should forget her position?"

"But how can I?" he asked, bewildered. "She is who she is. She can never be otherwise."

"But who *is* she?"

He gave her a wary look, as if wondering whether she had taken leave of her senses.

He replied very firmly,

"She is the Lady Violet Castleforde, only daughter of the tenth Duke of Castleforde and sister of the eleventh."

"Aha!" Elvina said triumphantly. "You got the last bit right."

"I got it completely right, madam."

"But your emphasis is mistaken and that is as bad as getting the facts wrong."

"I will not pretend to be able to follow your drift."

"All right, tell me this. Do you love Violet?"

"Of course I do."

"How much?"

She thought he was going to give her an angry reply, but after a moment his shoulders sagged and he said,

"Yes, very much."

"Splendid. Then we know her true identity. She is your much-loved sister. Not the Lady Violet, not the descendent of statesmen and grandees, but your sister whom you love."

There was a long silence, during which she saw his face soften and understanding dawn.

"I see," he said at last. "Yes, I begin to see,"

"Cannot you simply appreciate her for what she is?"

"I cannot cope with what she is," he responded ruefully.

"Come, you are His Grace the Duke of Castleforde," she coaxed with a laugh. "You are not going to admit that a sixteen year old girl could get the better of you, are you?"

"She gets the better of me whether I admit it or not," he said gloomily.

"Then don't let it be a battle," Elvina advised gently. "That can hurt her too badly."

She saw his surprise and thought she understood it. He was so often on the receiving end of Violet's temper that he had forgotten that she was still a vulnerable child.

"You understand her, don't you?" he asked.

"I think so. At any rate, I believe she will tolerate me for a while."

"How did you manage that miracle?"

"By not making it too obvious that I understand her," she replied mysteriously.

He frowned.

"Can you explain?"

"Would you really like to feel that someone could understand you through and through? I do not think so. It would make you feel as though you had no secrets left."

"Surely Violet doesn't have secrets at her age?"

"Everyone has secrets, Your Grace. Violet keeps thoughts to herself she tells nobody for she has nobody to tell."

"She could confide in me."

Elvina did not answer directly, but regarded him with her head on one side.

"No, I suppose she cannot confide in me," he added with a sigh.

"You have no idea how she longs for your love and approval. How can you have when she doesn't know it herself? She must be treated gently."

"Now I know *your* secret," he probed.

"You – do?"

He gave her a faint, disturbing smile.

"You are a most unexpected woman with hidden talents. I predict that you are going to turn my house and maybe my life upside down."

"You give me too much credit, sir. I am only a governess."

"I don't think so. I think you are far more than a governess. What will happen next, I wonder?"

CHAPTER FOUR

The air seemed to sing in Elvina's ears. The Duke had said,

"What will happen next, I wonder?"

And for an instant it really seemed as though something momentous was about to happen.

But then the strange mood broke. The butler entered the room, standing back to allow Violet to pass.

The Duke, who had been looking at Elvina, turned round and stared in astonishment.

He did not at first recognise his sister, who appeared sparkling from head to foot. Then, as she moved towards him, he stared harder.

"Violet?" he asked eventually.

At precisely the right moment she swept him a low curtsy.

"My Lord Duke," she declared theatrically.

Then suddenly the Duke laughed.

"Can it really be you?" he asked. "You look so lovely, just as I want you to look. I only wish we were going to a ball tonight. You would be undoubtedly the Belle of the Ball."

"Thank you, Your Grace," Violet purred demurely.

"What caused this change?" he demanded.

"I thought it was what you wanted, that I should be preparing myself for my debut. I am sure you have said so."

"Yes, and you have said that Society is for fools."

"She said no such thing," Elvina stopped him firmly. "You misheard her. All that matters now is that Violet looks wonderful and you know that she will be a credit to you."

Suddenly the butler announced from the door,

"Dinner is served, Your Grace."

The Duke hesitated for a moment.

Then he offered his arm to Elvina and his other arm to his sister.

"I never expected," he said, "that tonight would be a very special night. Perhaps we will continue to be able to talk comfortably amongst ourselves."

He smiled as he added,

"But another time when you are looking so beautiful, we must have a crowd of people to admire you, which unfortunately they have not done up to now."

They were walking along the corridor to the dining room as he finished speaking.

"I would love a ball," Violet volunteered, "and everything I have not had before. Quite frankly we have a lot to learn before other people come in to stare at us."

The Duke looked so surprised that Elvina's eyes twinkled.

Then he asked,

"Is this really my sister who is telling me that she wants parties? Is this also my sister who looks so beautiful that she will be the Belle of every ball?"

Violet laughed.

"Yes, this is your sister," she replied. "But as you want me to learn, so I am learning. Some of the things I am learning might surprise you, but you might also be pleased."

"Of course I will be," her brother said. "How has this magical witch come down to us just when we needed her?"

He was looking at Elvina as he spoke and she smiled back at him.

"I have been called many names, but a magical witch is something new," she sighed.

"I am astonished that my sister can look so lovely," the Duke continued. "I hope this is not just a dream and that I shall wake up to find that things are as bad as they used to be."

"Forget it! Forget the past," Elvina cried. "We are entering a new world, a world in which we dream up new ideas and learn so much which has never been learnt before. Eventually we will find a happiness which everyone seeks but few people are fortunate enough to find."

The Duke gazed at her.

"Are you really saying this to me?" he asked. "I am sure I am dreaming."

"It is as true as true can be," Elvina answered. "You must admit your sister looks absolutely lovely."

"How is it possible that you have waved a magic wand and made such a transformation?"

"The magic wand is at your service, Your Grace, so do not forget it's there when you need it. As it belongs to me, I will be there too!"

"That *is* a relief," the Duke responded at once. "I should be very upset if you leave us after all this."

Violet's eyes sparkled. She looked at Elvina who was sitting on the other side of her.

"I told you he would be surprised," she whispered.

51

"If I am dreaming," the Duke said before Elvina could speak, "I have no intention of waking up. Not until we have enjoyed some parties, at any rate."

"Before we have too many parties," Elvina broke in quickly, "I would love to see your horses."

She laughed and preened herself. "I am considered an expert, you know. My father bred horses and they were in demand all over the countryside."

"Your father was a horse-breeder?" the Duke asked, with a little emphasis of surprise.

Elvina guessed that to him a horse-breeder was a rough, unlettered man and since she was obviously a gentlewoman he could make no connection.

"He never call himself a horse-breeder," she explained quickly. "He was the younger son of a – well, of a good family."

"So I would have supposed, madam," he said quietly.

"And I loved horses as much as he did. It was quite a partnership."

"Until you met your husband," Violet queried.

"Until I – ? Oh, yes, until I met my husband."

"And what did your husband think about horses?" the Duke asked.

"He loved them too. He was an ex-army man," Elvina improvised. She knew she was borrowing details from Andrew and she wished that she need not do so, but she was in too much of a flurry to think too far ahead.

"Ah! Cavalry?" the Duke enquired.

"Yes. Of course, people don't think that women know anything about horses."

"But you intend to surprise us," the Duke said with a smile that made his face full of charm.

He began to tell them tales of his own horses, some of which were quite amusing, such as the time he had set his heart on a particular horse and had been cheated out of it at the last minute.

"The trouble," he said, "is that there are far too many people wanting too few horses, as you have doubtless found."

He looked at Elvina as he continued,

"If the horses are exceptional, there are so many people trying to buy them that the price rises minute after minute until only a millionaire could afford them."

"That is exactly what I heard my father say. But he used to manage, in some clever way of his own, to see the horses before they appeared in the sales yard, rather than after a great number of bidders had realised their value."

"That is the sensible thing to do," he agreed. "But unfortunately one is not always so lucky. I paid far too much for the last two animals I bought, simply because they had been talked about."

"One cannot always be lucky when it comes to money."

"You need to be wealthy to start with to afford a decent stable."

She spoke without thinking and was taken aback when the Duke remarked,

"You talk as if yours is a large and expensive collection. Surely I must have heard of it."

Elvina realised that she had made a slip. Quickly she added, "I have known many clients with large stables. They were always boasting that they were their most expensive possession."

The Duke laughed and nodded. But there was an expression in his eyes which told her he was still finding her difficult to understand.

He was undoubtedly questioning why she was here and how she could have owned the attractive dress which she had lent Violet as well as her own.

To change the subject, Elvina began to talk about music.

She asked the Duke if he had heard the new tunes which were currently such a success in London and if there was a music room in the castle.

"There is one which has been here for many years," the Duke told her. "You did not mention whether you could play the piano, but somehow I feel quite certain that you can."

"I can play the piano and I love music. I am certain your sister loves it too. One day we must have a musical evening. Do you play any instrument, Your Grace?"

"I used to play a violin, but I am out of practise."

"But you could start to practise again. If your sister and I play the piano and sing with you playing the violin, we can have a musical evening which we should all enjoy. I am sure your neighbours would enjoy it too."

"Invite other people? Heaven forbid!" he exclaimed in horror.

"Have you never played for an audience? If not, there is hardly any point in learning an instrument."

"When I was a child I sometimes performed at my parents' insistence, to please their friends. Although just how much pleasure it gave them to hear me scraping away, is doubtful. But now – "

Elvina decided to take a risk.

"But now it's different," she said. "Now you are a great man and you do not have to worry about pleasing other people."

Violet giggled. Her brother glared at her.

Then he scowled at Elvina, but she faced him with a challenging look.

"I question how pleasing my playing would be to anyone," he asserted through gritted teeth. "Unless, of course, it amused them. If you imagine I am exposing myself to ridicule, you are much mistaken."

"Well, we will just have to see how musical you still are when we are on our own."

He did not reply, although his face became a little less grim as he regarded her wryly.

"Is your piano in good condition?" she asked. "Perhaps you should buy a new one."

"You are running me into debt, even before you have been here for one day!"

"The Lady Violet Castleforde deserves nothing less than the best if she is to succeed," Elvina retorted.

The Duke raised his head and regarded her, almost as though wondering if she would dare to tease him.

"And are *you* a good pianist, Mrs. Winters?" he asked.

"In some respects."

"In that case, when we have finished eating, we will go to the music room and you will play and sing for us. Then you can give me your opinion of the piano."

Elvina wanted to say, "*touché!*" But she merely contented herself with a smile.

55

Although it was summer the evening air was chilly and Elvina was glad to see a fire burning in the music room, casting its glow over the oak furniture and the magnificent piano.

As soon as she ran her fingers over the keys, she knew that the piano was in perfect condition. She looked up and caught the Duke watching her, a gleam of humour in his eyes.

When she gave him an answering smile he laughed out loud.

"I keep it perfectly tuned," he admitted, "because even my sister practises sometimes."

"I have been trying to learn some of the new songs from London," Violet joined in, adding daringly, "they sing them on the stage."

"Indeed?" remarked the Duke, refusing to be provoked.

Elvina was looking through the song sheets.

"I have been learning this one," Violet said eagerly, pointing to the sheet of music in Elvina's hand. The song is called '*I Remember The Day*'."

"Have you ever played it, Mrs. Winters?" Violet wanted to know.

"Er – yes, but – "

"Oh, good, you can play and sing it now."

"I don't think – "

"Oh, but you must. Then you can show me how it should be done."

"That's right," the Duke echoed with a touch of mischief. "Show us how it should be done."

She would rather have sung any song but this one. It carried too many memories of evenings she had spent with Margaret and Andrew.

There had been one occasion, in particular, when she had sat at the piano, playing and singing this very song. They had been there with her, both smiling.

She had thought their smiles were for her. Now she realised that they must have been for each other, excluding her.

Violet was pulling out the stool for her. Reluctantly, but having no choice, Elvina sat down and played the opening bars. Then she began to sing in a soft, sweet voice,

"I remember the day,
When first I met him,
The sun in his Heaven,
All well in the world.
I remember the day,
When we first walked together,
My hand held in his,
And the love in his eyes."

She had thought she had seen love in Andrew's eyes and it had all been a delusion. The memory overwhelmed her with grief and suddenly her voice thickened. She could sing no more.

"What is it?" Violet asked, jumping up in alarm.

"Nothing, I – I am a little husky tonight."

"I expect you are tired," the Duke said quietly. "There is no need for any more, Mrs. Winters. Clearly you are an accomplished musician."

He too rose and came towards her, taking her hand to raise her from the piano stool.

"It has been a long day for you, but now you belong here and I hope this day will be the first of many."

As he finished speaking, Violet threw up her arms.

"We have won! We have won!" she cried excitedly to Elvina. "You will stay and you and I will surprise everyone with our new ideas and new achievements."

She held out her hands towards Elvina who was on the other side of the Duke, who reached out his own hands to take them.

As they touched each other, Violet said to her brother,

"Now you are our prisoner and you cannot escape. We are going to cover you with new ideas, new experiences and new music. Will you give us a free hand?"

"Anything you want," he answered. "This is what I prayed and hoped would happen, but felt was impossible."

He turned to Elvina,

"I will do everything in my power to prevent you from leaving."

There was a note in his voice which Elvina thought rather moving.

As she met his eyes she thought what he was saying to her privately was something she dare not admit, even to herself.

*

The next morning Elvina rose early and walked into Violet's room. The girl had just left her bed and was standing by the window, looking out on the sunny scene. Her eyes lit up when she saw that Elvina was dressed for riding.

"I was hoping that's what we would be doing," she said. "It is such a lovely morning. Let's go at once."

"We will have some breakfast first, if you please, and while we are alone, I have something to say to you."

"Yes?" Violet asked demurely.

"Behave yourself. Last night you made some very pointed remarks and it will not do. You promised you would keep my secret."

"But it's not my fault," Violet protested. "How can anyone believe in you as a governess? You don't look as if you need to earn your own living, and you have such wonderful clothes they could only belong to someone who could afford to buy them."

Elvina held up her hands.

"Hush! Hush!" she exclaimed. "You must not say that. You may think it, but do not say it in front of your brother."

"You are making me more curious as to who you really are," Violet ventured. "You are so clever. Just think of everything you have managed to do since you arrived. My brother thinks you are marvellous, the servants are impressed and the music room is being opened for us."

"And you," Elvina interrupted, "are going to be exactly what your brother wants you to be. So count your blessings and not mine."

Violet laughed.

"I think it is impossible to separate them," she said. "I was just lying in bed and thinking how exciting it is to have you here and how different I feel this morning from other mornings."

They breakfasted alone and ate quickly, eager to go to the stables.

Violet's mount was a white mare with a gentle expression. Elvina admired her beauty but for herself she preferred a more spirited animal.

When she had studied every animal in the stables, Elvina said,

"I like the grey stallion. He looks powerful."

"You would like to ride Joby?" Violet asked, giving her a sidelong glance.

"I should like it above everything."

Violet went in search of a groom and came back with a young man, instructing him to bring a lady's saddle for the stallion. It took him a few minutes to do so, as Joby was skittish and disinclined to obey.

At last Elvina was able to mount him, hopping nimbly across his back before he could object. Through her firm hold on the reins, she let him know that he would be wasting his time giving her trouble and he seemed to understand.

Together Violet and Elvina rode out into the paddock, starting to gallop as soon as they were in the field beyond.

Then they gave the horses their heads. On and on they galloped, with Elvina having to rein Joby in to prevent him racing too far ahead of Violet's mare.

When eventually they slowed to a halt, Elvina looked around and realised that they had come several miles.

"Violet," Elvina asked sternly, "who normally rides this stallion?"

"Well – nobody," Violet said awkwardly. "Nobody except the groom, that is. And David, of course. He has only just bought him, and – "

"What have you done to me, you wretched girl?" Elvina groaned. "Are you trying to have me sent away?"

"But I was sure you were good enough to ride him. David is so superior about women riders. But perhaps we had better not tell him."

"That will be quite unnecessary," Elvina said, pointing into the distance with her whip.

Violet followed the direction and gasped at the sight of her brother galloping towards them on a fine black steed. Even from a distance they could see his scowl and had no doubt what had annoyed him.

"Hallo, David," Violet called brightly.

He ignored her.

"Mrs. Winters," he said curtly, "will you please tell me what you are doing on the back of a horse I have strictly forbidden anyone but an experienced groom to ride?

"David, please it was my – "

"Be silent!" he commanded Violet. "In fact I need no explanation. I will not tolerate insubordination. Mrs. Winters, please pack your things and leave my premises at once."

Elvina's temper flared.

"I will not!" she snapped. "I never heard of anything so unjust in all my life. I had no idea of your prohibition."

"My decision is made. Please leave."

"You can't do that," Violet cried. "It was all my fault."

"My dear girl, what's one governess, more or less. You send them away pretty fast yourself. Now I am sending this one away."

"But Mrs. Winters is different," Violet pleaded. "I want to keep her, *I really do*."

"In that case you had better treat her a bit better than you have this morning," the Duke cautioned her calmly.

61

Elvina gave him a wry smile. She had detected a gleam in his eye a moment earlier. In fact, she could almost have sworn that he winked at her. Whether he did or not, she had guessed he was up to something.

"Wh-what?" Violet stammered.

"You know better than to allow Mrs. Winters to ride that horse," he told her. "I don't know what you were playing at – a joke at my expense, perhaps."

"Well, Mrs. Winters can ride as well as any man."

"But you didn't know that. You say you value her, but you took a risk you had no right to take. I thought I would teach you a lesson about the consequences."

"You never meant a word of it," Violet cried. "I think you are horrid."

"We both are. Mrs. Winters, my apologies. I accept that none of this was your fault. I hope you can find it in your heart to forgive me."

"I will give it my earnest consideration," she replied gravely.

Elvina was slightly irked by his cool assumption that a few words would win his forgiveness.

He shot her a shrewd look.

"You are still offended with me. Well, perhaps I have deserved it. Allow me to compliment you on your riding. You held Joby as no other woman and few men could have done."

"Thank you, Your Grace."

"Of course, galloping with Violet is easy. Could you gallop against me, riding this brute? No, no, forget I said that. It wasn't fair."

There was only one possible answer and Elvina gave it, digging her heel into Joby's side and streaming away before he had finished speaking.

The Duke had just time to shout, "stay here" to his sister and then he was after Elvina, striving to close the lead she had already gained.

Elvina heard him gaining ground behind her and urged Joby on faster and faster. He was a powerful steed, but not quite as fast as the Duke's great black stallion.

Suddenly filled with exhilaration, Elvina gave Joby his head. Inch by inch she began to draw away, but the Duke closed the gap again.

She could hear him. Then, turning her head a little, she glanced over her shoulder and saw his face, tense with effort.

Elvina laughed. In the joy of riding a fine horse to the limit everything else was forgotten.

Then his expression changed to one full of horror. She heard his hoarse cry of "*look out!*"

Too late she swung her head round to the front. The wall that she should have seen had come upon her suddenly. Joby had seen it and gathered himself for the jump.

Elvina leaned forward, trying to adjust her position at the last minute, but the jump was unusually high and Joby was already starting to soar.

Unable to centre herself in the saddle in time, Elvina slipped sideways as the wall glided beneath her and the next moment she was falling into the unknown.

CHAPTER FIVE

The world spun violently around Elvina. Trees and ground seemed to merge into one blurred whole. From somewhere she heard a terrified cry of "*no!*" before she crashed into something solid and darkness descended.

She opened her eyes to find that the world was still going round although less fiercely. She was lying on the ground being held up by a strong pair of arms.

Looking up she saw the Duke's lean face gazing down at her with an expression of horror in his dark eyes.

"Mrs. Winters," he whispered. "Can you hear me?"

"Yes," she murmured.

She tried to move, but immediately his arms tightened.

"Keep still," he said. "Help is on its way. Luckily Violet ignored my order to remain where she was. She followed at a distance, saw what happened and galloped off for help."

Elvina managed a faint smile.

"I wonder what she'll bring back."

"I see you already know her well, madam. Yes, she is quite capable of returning with her maid and a piece of sticking plaster, but I hope she will find a doctor for you."

"I don't – need a doctor. I have taken falls before."

"Not like this. You landed on stones."

"Is that why I ache all over?"

"I should think more than very likely," he said with careful restraint. "Also, your head is bleeding."

"You must be very angry with me," she muttered vaguely.

"I ought to be for such an act of madness. What were you thinking of, apart from getting the better of me?"

"I think that must have been it," she admitted, managing a smile.

"Mrs. Winters, you are quite outrageous," the Duke said. But he spoke gently.

The next moment they heard the welcome sound of a horse and the Duke called out,

"Over here."

It was the doctor in his pony and trap.

"I met Lady Violet on the road," he said, "and she sent me here. She also charged me to tell you that she has ridden back to the house to despatch a carriage to convey Mrs. Winters in comfort."

"Excellent," the Duke said. "She has shown more good sense than I would have expected of her."

"Tell her so," Elvina murmured. Unthinkingly she clasped his hand in hers. "You *must* tell her so."

He looked startled, but did not withdraw his hand.

"I will," he agreed.

"No bones broken," the doctor said at last. "You are very lucky not to have broken them all on these stones."

"Is it safe to lift her?" the Duke asked.

"Quite safe."

Within a few minutes the carriage had arrived. The Duke helped Elvina gently to her feet and lifted her in. Tying their horses to the rear, they began the slow journey back to the house.

For all that journey the Duke held Elvina steady, with one arm about her and her head on his shoulder.

She could have cried out with mortification that her display of daring had ended in this way. But at the same time, she became aware of a feeling of safety and contentment, even though she ached all over.

Having arranged for the carriage, Violet had gone into the house to alert the housekeeper. Now she came out onto the top step to witness their approach and dash back inside, crying, "they're here! They're here!"

Then they had stopped and the Duke was lifting her out in his strong arms, carrying her into the house and up the stairs to her room.

There the women took over, undressing her, putting her to bed and waiting with her while the doctor looked at her more closely before cleaning and dressing the cut on her forehead.

"You are going to be covered in bruises," he informed her. "But it will be no worse than that. You need plenty of rest, so stay in bed."

He repeated all this to the Duke in the corridor outside.

"But you will call again tomorrow?" the Duke enquired.

"If that is what Your Grace wishes, although there is really no need – "

"That is what I wish," he replied firmly.

"Very well, Your Grace. I have administered a sleeping draught to Mrs. Winters and left another for the maid to give her later tonight."

"My sister will attend to her. I will see you tomorrow, doctor."

The doctor inclined his head and departed. The Duke looked up to find Violet staring at him in amazement.

Before he could say anything she gave a little chuckle and darted back into Elvina's bedroom.

*

For two days Elvina stayed in bed, mostly sleeping.

Then one morning she awoke feeling well and strong. As the doctor had predicted, she was covered in bruises, but she had been bruised before and could cope.

The Duke and Violet seemed to feel that she was made of glass and must be protected. After the first two days they allowed her to get up, but only as far as to come downstairs to a sunny room where French windows opened onto the gardens.

"I don't deserve all this care," she told the Duke. "To cause so much trouble on my first day – "

"But the fault was mine," he interrupted her. "You forget that I dared you. That was a shocking thing to do and had you been killed your death would have been on my conscience. It is I who should ask for your forgiveness."

"Then I give it gladly," she replied. "Riding Joby was an experience that I would not have missed for the world, except for the last part. And even that would not have happened if he and I had known each other better, or if I had known your land. Next time it will be different."

"Next time will never happen," he intervened hastily. "I will find you a gentle mare to ride."

"Thank you," she responded in a lifeless voice.

In truth the Duke was rather shocked at himself. Mrs. Winters, however admirable, was a servant. From birth he had been accustomed to regard servants as a different kind of creature, living on the other side of a barrier which could never be crossed. It was not intentional arrogance, simply what a man of his class had been reared to consider normal.

He was a good Master, even a kind and considerate one. He paid generous wages and employed more servants than he needed so that none should be over-worked.

Yet with all his kindness, he had always regarded his employees as a separate breed. They were like children to him. It was his duty to care for them, but the idea of treating them as equals had never entered his mind.

To a man who thought in this way the idea of issuing a challenge to a servant and a female servant at that was simply unthinkable. Yet he had found himself doing so, driven on by something about Mrs. Winters that was different, not only from others who worked for him, but from other women.

Already he knew it was essential to keep her at the castle for Violet's sake, yet he had taken an insane risk with her safety. And he could not quite understand what had made him behave in a manner so unlike himself.

Over the next few days he began to drop in on her as she reclined on the sofa in the sunny room where she was now resting.

In fact, her vigour was fast returning and only a direct command from the Duke prevented her from heading for the stables.

Violet spent almost all her time with Elvina and the Duke told himself that, as Violet's brother and guardian, he must know what was being taught. It therefore became his duty to spend time with the two of them in the sunny room, listening in fascination and occasionally laughing.

They were strange lessons, he thought, unlike any he had ever heard before – almost like two young women gossiping.

And yet he was wise enough to notice that Violet enjoyed being with her governess almost more than any other occupation. And that could only be good, he reasoned.

Once he found them reading Hamlet together.

"However did you persuade her to sit still for Shakespeare?" he demanded when Violet had left the room for a moment.

"But of course she wants to read Shakespeare?" Elvina replied with an air of surprise. "It is essential for a future actress."

"But I have already informed you that a girl in Violet's position – "

Then he saw Elvina regarding him with her head on one side, a knowing smile on her lovely mouth and he relaxed.

"Of course," he said. "You are being clever, as I should have known that you would be."

"Hamlet's advice to the players was very useful," she told him. "But of course, Lady Violet could not read that advice on its own. It was necessary for her to understand Hamlet's state of mind and why he put on the play – "

"For which she had to read the rest of the play," he finished.

"Of course. And from there we will proceed to other works by Shakespeare," Elvina said. "Although I am much tempted to make her read *The Duchess of Malfi*. I think she would enjoy it."

"I haven't read it, madam, but from the way you are looking at me I fear the worst!"

"It is about a young woman whose life is made a misery by a tyrannical brother," Elvina said demurely. "She will appreciate that story!"

69

There was a silence and then the Duke burst out laughing. But suddenly he stopped and a confused look came over his face.

"You must teach her whatever you wish," he said abruptly. "I trust you completely."

He hurried out of the room, leaving Elvina staring after him puzzled.

She did not know that he had shocked himself by laughing so freely with her. Worse, his eyes had sought hers, seeking in them the warmth of shared humour.

It had made him flee.

But he returned later that day, entering quietly while Elvina was talking to Violet. He seated himself without interrupting them and listened.

Elvina was not teaching facts, but advising on behaviour. And Violet he was fascinated to observe was listening intently.

"But I am sure you are clever enough to make people not only admire you, but love you because you are you," Elvina was saying.

There was silence for a moment as Violet considered this idea before asking,

"Do you mean that? Do you really think people might – might *like* me?"

"Of course they will like you," Elvina replied. "Just as I think you are charming and delightful and very amusing."

"Amusing?" the Duke asked with a slight frown.

Absorbed in each other, neither of them had noticed him. Now they smiled and Violet pulled out a chair for him to join them.

"I was just telling Lady Violet," Elvina said, "that she is going to be a great success."

She took Violet's hand.

"And the most important thing is to be sure that people admire you and love you because you are sweet and nice to them."

"It isn't always easy to be sweet and nice," Violet commented darkly.

"Of course," Elvina said. "If it was easy it would not be worth the effort."

"Violet," the Duke suggested, "why don't you go and ask cook to send us all some tea?"

Since he would normally never send his sister on an errand that properly belonged to a footman, both of them recognised that he wished to be alone with Elvina. Violet departed without protest.

Once they were alone the Duke smiled at Elvina.

"I like to hear my sister praised," he said. "But is this your idea of lessons?"

"Oh, yes," she replied seriously. "I am teaching her to think well of herself and that is a vital lesson."

"Think well of herself?" he echoed incredulously. "A young woman in her position is taught to think well of herself from her first moment."

"Not at all," Elvina said. "She is taught to think well of her title and position, not herself. One day she will find love and how lonely she will be if she cannot believe the man loves her for herself alone.

"I know she is socially important. But I don't think anyone has ever warned her that, because of her position, she will find it harder to win affection for her own self. And it is so easy – " she drew in a sharp breath, "so fatally easy to believe what one wants to believe."

"Yes," the Duke nodded slowly. "Yes, I think I understand."

"Do you? I suppose a Duke must often be the focus of matchmakers, concerned only with his title and riches."

"That is true. But I was thinking of something else. I am afraid my mother married my father for that kind of reason. She was a woman of fashion, who spent as much time in London as possible.

"She loved Society and for a while was a Lady-in-Waiting to the Queen. Jewels and clothes were all she cared about. She seldom bothered to be a mother to her daughter, and she would certainly never have taught Violet to value her character rather than her title."

"And that has left her sadly unprepared for Society," Elvina remarked. "It is not enough for your sister to have an unassailable standing in Society. I want her to be happy as well.

"Tell me, did you ever remember to praise her for the splendid way she fetched help on the day of my accident?"

The Duke made a sharp sound of annoyance with himself.

"No, with everything that happened it went completely out of my mind."

"Your praise and approval would mean so much to her."

"I shall make up for it at dinner tonight. You shall join us and hear how well I do."

"Thank you, I shall look forward to it."

"You are right, of course. I must admit, she sounded so amazed at the idea of being liked that it made me feel – " he stopped suddenly and his eye fell on a magazine open on the table beside Elvina.

"*The Debutante's Friend,*" he growled, revolted. "We discussed this earlier and I made my feelings clear."

"Yes, we did, and *I* made *my* feelings clear as well," Elvina returned with spirit.

"*What?*"

"Your Grace is simply mistaken."

"*I* am mistaken? Did I hear you correctly?"

"Perfectly. Soon Lady Violet will be going into a world of young men, seeking a suitable husband."

"You amaze me, I understood that she was going to be an actress."

"No, no, she only *thinks* she is going to be an actress. Do try to keep up."

"I – ?"

Sensing that she had gone a little too far, Elvina hurried on.

"I am afraid the melancholy truth is that most young men do not demand intelligence in a girl. If she appears ignorant, far from putting them off, it may make her more attractive."

"That cannot be true," he said, appalled.

"Sadly, it is. There are men who prefer a really stupid wife."

"Good Heavens! Why?"

"I suppose she might be less inclined to ask awkward questions about what he has been up to?" Elvina answered demurely.

For a moment he stared at her. Then his lips twitched faintly. But he controlled them.

"If you want to laugh, you should go ahead," Elvina said. "Of course there are some instincts that should be controlled, but laughter is seldom one of them."

He relaxed and allowed himself to grin.

"Now you mention it, I know men exactly like that," he admitted. "But I should hate my sister to marry any of them."

He was pacing the room and for a moment he was standing in the French window, silhouetted by the sun.

But then he whirled round suddenly and shot out a question.

"Is that what *you* did?"

Caught off-guard, she gasped, "I – ?"

"Did you marry a man who preferred a stupid wife? Tell me about Mr. Winters."

With horror, she realised that she should have prepared herself for this moment. Suddenly her mind had gone blank.

"Oh – well – he – "

To hide her confusion she rose from the sofa and turned away, covering her face with her hands.

The Duke saw the gesture and misunderstood it.

"My dear lady, do forgive me," he said quickly. "I did not mean to upset you. I assumed you are a widow – "

"Yes," she replied, pulling herself together quickly. "That's right, I'm – I'm a widow."

He moved closer to her and put an arm about her shoulders.

"Has your husband been dead for long?"

"A year," she said, improvising quickly.

"And it still hurts you to talk about him. Please try to forgive me."

The gentleness in his voice was almost her undoing. She felt swamped with guilt for deceiving him when he was being so kind. But it was too late to back out now.

"Please think nothing of it. It was just that you caught me by surprise."

"But you grieve for him still?" the Duke enquired, in the same gentle voice, laying his other hand on her shoulder.

"Please do not ask me to talk about him," she said hurriedly.

"Of course."

He looked into her face.

"I treat you very badly, don't I?"

"Oh, no, you are kinder than I deserve."

"I am very sure than I am not," he added with a touch of sadness in his voice.

Then to her amazement and perhaps his own, he drew her close to him and laid his lips against her forehead.

She stared at him, shaken to the soul. For a moment his mouth seemed very near and her heart began to beat faster.

Then a sudden noise from outside startled them.

Elvina turned away quickly, one instant before Violet came in with a housemaid bearing tea.

"Here we are," Violet announced. "Tea for everybody!"

"Not for me," the Duke muttered hastily. "I must be going."

Violet turned in dismay. "But – "

"I will see you both at dinner," he threw over his shoulder as he left the room.

"I thought he meant to stay with us for a while," Violet said. "I wonder what made him run away."

"Your brother is a very busy man," Elvina replied quietly. "This tea looks lovely."

She did not want to talk further of what had happened.

But had anything happened?

Surely the fleeting moment had been all in her imagination?

Besides, what could it possibly mean?

"Mrs. Winters?" Violet asked, looking at her in alarm.

"I'm sorry – what?"

"You were off in a dream."

"Was I? Then the sooner I have some tea the better."

After that, nothing further was said on the subject.

*

Elvina had not dined with the Duke and Violet since the first evening, but now she was officially well again and that night she dressed with care.

The gown she chose was deep pink, embroidered with roses. Around her neck she wore one strand of pearls and she dressed her hair in the plainest style she could manage.

When the time came she and Violet walked downstairs together. As they entered the drawing room, the Duke's eyes flickered over her.

"My compliments on your recovery, madam," he began. "Violet, does she not look well?"

"I think she looks wonderful," Violet enthused.

"And much of the credit for such a good recovery must go to you," he told her warmly. "You displayed great presence of mind that day. In all the upset I neglected to tell you so, but I was very proud of you."

The look Violet turned on him was so blissful and yet so startled that he was taken aback.

What Mrs. Winters had told him was true, he realised. It was his affection that Violet yearned for. And all the while he had only offered her endless rules.

He then further amazed her by kissing her cheek and leading her to the dinner table.

Over dinner he made several joking references to *The Duchess of Malfi,* calling on Elvina to back him up.

Violet later said that she had never seen him so pleasant.

Eventually he said,

"I have to go away for a few days. Mrs. Winters, can I trust you not to take out any of my dangerous horses?"

"None of your horses are dangerous to me," she protested sweetly.

"Your accident shows otherwise, madam."

"Ah, but I shall be prepared for Joby next time. If I just –"

"You will not mount Joby now or ever. I forbid it. Now give me your word or before Heaven I will not leave."

Elvina started, struck by some strange tone in his voice even more than by his forceful words.

"Of course I give you my word," she agreed. "But I only wish I had my own favourite horses here with me. Now they are *really* horses!" she added provocatively.

He eyed her askance.

"Then why don't you bring some of your animals here and let me judge them for myself. I will house and feed them at no charge to you."

Suddenly she was overwhelmed with longing to see her favourites again. If only she dared –

Of course there would be danger in writing home and telling somebody where she was. But she knew one person whom she could trust absolutely not to reveal anything.

"I would love to," she said. "Thank you so much – Your Grace."

She had to catch herself up a little on the last words. As the daughter of an Earl, it would have been permissible for her to address him simply as 'Duke' and there were several Dukes of her acquaintance with whom she did exactly that.

But as mere Mrs. Winters she must observe the correct formality. The problem was that in the last few days she had felt herself growing closer to him and it was becoming harder to be cautious.

She spent the rest of that day writing a letter to Simpson, the head groom in her stables. He was an old retainer and should have been pensioned off years ago but he had fiercely resisted the idea.

He had been devoted to Elvina's father and was now devoted to her. He was the one man whom she could trust with her story, partly because he was completely reliable and also partly because of another attribute.

Elvina's lips curved into a smile as she thought of his other attribute and how useful it would be now.

Having given Simpson his instructions, she wrote a banker's draft that would provide him with enough money to bring her horses across country, staying in hotels where the stables were good.

She enclosed the letter in an envelope and then put that into another envelope, which she addressed to the landlord of *The Dragon,* an inn in the village near her estate.

In a separate letter she asked the landlord to send a boy to Simpson and deliver the enclosed to him. This too she placed in the envelope and sent for a footman to put it in the post.

All anyone here would see was that she had written to someone at *The Dragon.* They could wonder, but they would not guess the truth.

Now there was nothing to do but wait. Elvina began to calculate how long it would take for her letter to arrive and then how long it would take for Simpson to bring the two horses to her.

When would he be here? When?

If she only knew exactly where he had gone! But he had not told her. He had only said that he must leave for a few days –

With a start, Elvina came to herself and realised that her mind had slipped sideways.

She was no longer thinking of Simpson, but of the Duke. It was his absence that concerned her.

When would he return?

When?

CHAPTER SIX

Three days later, while reading *Romeo and Juliet* with Violet in the library, Elvina was informed by an agitated footman that she had a visitor.

The young footman told her, wooden-faced, that the newcomer was a rough, rude man who spoke in grunts, demanded to see Mrs. Winters and otherwise refused to give any account of himself.

Elvina chuckled, recognising Simpson from the graphic description.

"Wait here a moment," she told Violet.

"Can I not come with you?"

"Certainly not. While I am away you can learn Juliet's potion speech and act it for me when I return."

She ran down to the stables and her eyes lit up with delight at the sight of Jupiter and Mars, her two dearest steeds.

And there, too, was the friendly, familiar face of Simpson, looking as though it was carved out of oak. He was about sixty, tall and sturdy.

He had served Elvina's family all his life and was not in the least surprised that she had finally recognised that she could not do without him. Not before time, in his opinion.

"Good morning, Mrs. Winters," he greeted her, remembering his instructions.

Elvina welcomed him, then spoke to Harris, who ran the Duke's stables and who was studying Jupiter and Mars with admiration.

"Two of the finest beasts it's been my privilege to see, ma'am," he said. "His Grace told me they were coming and that they were to be well housed. And if Mr. Simpson would like to lodge with Mrs. Harris and me, we have a very nice room."

He looked expectantly at Simpson as he spoke, but receiving no response, he became puzzled.

"Simpson is a little hard of hearing," Elvina explained.

Harris said it all again louder and this time the matter was resolved.

Once she had seen her horses stabled and fed, Elvina took a stroll with her groom to the little wood nearby, where they could be sure of privacy. For it was true that he was a little deaf, although not nearly so deaf as he sometimes assumed.

"How are things at home?" she asked, as casually as she could.

"Goin' well," he assured her. "The butler thanks you for the banker's draft and the horses are all in prime condition."

"And my neighbours? Is there any local gossip?"

"One matter that may interest my La– that is, may interest you, ma'am. Captain Broadmoor and Miss Margaret have announced their engagement."

The world seemed to stop. Elvina told herself not to be absurd. She had half expected this news. And yet –

"That is most interesting," she said, trying to sound bright. "And very suitable."

"Indeed, ma'am. I must say that some of us were disappointed, havin' hoped that the Captain and yourself – "

"Oh, no," she replied quickly. "There was never any question of that. I always encouraged him to court Margaret. I am delighted for them."

Simpson had brought all the mail that had arrived since her departure and a brief glance told Elvina that one of the envelopes was addressed in Andrew's hand.

"Thank you," she said in a colourless voice. "Why don't you go and settle into your lodgings now?"

"Yes, ma'am."

He walked off, leaving her glowering at the envelope.

At last she forced herself to open it and stared amazed at the contents,

'Dear Lady Elvina,

I do not know what good angel prompted you to give me two thousand pounds just before I announced my engagement, but I can only say that you have my heartfelt thanks.

Miss Halson has honoured me by consenting to be my wife and your wedding gift will give us the perfect start in life.

Thank you from both of us.

Your devoted friend,

Andrew Broadmoor.'

Whatever she had expected, it was not this cool formal acceptance of her bounty, as though whatever life offered him was no more than his due. The sheer effrontery of the letter made her gasp.

She had made a lucky escape. And yet this dismal ending to what had been such high hopes cast a blight over her heart, and she found herself weeping despite her good sense.

In the library Violet closed her eyes and tried to remember the words she was learning.

"I have a faint, cold fear that runs through my veins."

"What's this?"

Violet opened her eyes at the unexpected voice.

"David!" she cried, beaming and running to hug him.

When they had exchanged greetings he asked,

"Where is Mrs. Winters?"

"Oh, David it is *such* fun. Someone has come to see her and she has gone to the stables to see him and she's being very mysterious."

"Then probably her horses have arrived. What is there to be mysterious about?"

"She wouldn't let me go with her."

"How sensible of her," he said with a grin. "I must go and reconnoitre. You stay here and do whatever Mrs. Winters told you to do."

"Spoil sport!"

He laughed and departed. He could not have said why he had refused to take her with him, but for some reason he wanted his meeting with Mrs. Winters to be just the two of them.

He walked first to the stables, where he found Simpson, who had just returned from talking to Elvina in the wood and greeted him in a friendly manner.

"So you work for Mrs. Winters?" he asked jovially. "I expect they are missing her at home."

Simpson turned blank eyes on him.

"A little hard of hearing, Your Grace," Harris murmured.

"You work for Mrs. Winters?" the Duke shouted.

"Yes, Your Grace," Simpson replied.

"In her stables?"

"Yes, Your Grace."

"Are they large stables?"

"Your Grace?"

The Duke sighed and gave up. There might be a chance to learn more of the mystery of Mrs. Winters, but this would not be it.

"Does anyone know where Mrs. Winters is?" he enquired.

"In the wood, Your Grace," said Simpson, displaying a remarkable sharpness for a man who had been deaf a moment before.

The Duke flung him a look and went off to the wood.

He wondered how he would find her. Beneath the trees, perhaps. He imagined how pretty she would look, wandering in and out of shafts of sunlight.

But when he came upon Elvina, he was taken completely by surprise. She was sitting on a fallen tree trunk, her face buried in her hands, weeping bitterly. An open letter lay at her feet.

"Good Heavens, what is the matter?"

He had moved to stand in front of her and his voice made her raise her head before she had the chance to control her emotions. He was shocked by the sight of tears pouring down her cheeks.

For a moment the mask with which she shielded herself from the world was gone, leaving her utterly defenceless.

"What is it?" he pleaded again. "For pity's sake, tell me."

Her answer was to glance down at the letter by her feet and snatch it up, crushing it between her fingers before he could see it.

"Why are you crying?" he demanded. "Tell me."

He sat down on the log beside her, putting his hands onto her shoulders.

"You must tell me," he urged her.

"There – is nothing to tell," she stammered.

"I do not believe you."

He heard her gulp and immediately said,

"Forgive me. I had no right to speak to you so."

"You have no right to question me either," she gasped.

A remarkable force seemed to stream from him, taking possession of her, so that she felt as if she had no choice but to confide in him.

And she must not do so. Nobody must know how stupid she had been.

"No, I have no right to question you," he agreed. "Your private affairs are not my concern. I only thought that there might be some way I could help."

"Nobody can help me. I was very foolish – and there is no help for that."

"Somehow I cannot imagine you being foolish," he pointed out gently. "You are such a strong woman, putting us all in order."

"Oh, no, I don't – "

"Do not contradict me, Mrs. Winters," he said, smiling. "I say that we are both in your debt, Violet and I. What will happen to us if you collapse?"

"I will *not* collapse," she asserted firmly.

"But who is there to help you, as you have been helping us?"

"I do not need any help. I had a moment's weakness, but it has passed. Now I am myself again."

With his hands still on her shoulders he searched her face.

"Yourself," he repeated. "But who is '*yourself?*' Who are you?"

"I am your sister's governess and no more."

"A governess who comes from another life, another world. You are a great deal more than a governess. Why do you weep alone and allow nobody to comfort you? Why do you hide from the world – *from me?*"

He had not meant to ask the final question and her face showed him that she was startled. She seemed to be looking at him imploringly. For a moment he appeared to hover in space. His hands gripped her shoulders tighter.

And then a bird flew overhead, its shadow touching their faces and the spell was broken.

His breath left him slowly as the dream seemed to leave him. She too felt herself return to reality. Something had happened, but she did not know what. The world was different.

"Forgive me," he said slowly. "I had no right to intrude into your private affairs. Your feelings are your own. They do not concern me."

He said the last words with a kind of desperation, like a man who was trying to convince himself.

"I am most grateful for your kindness," Elvina responded in measured tones. "But I should be getting back to my pupil. I have left her alone too long."

"Yes, I believe your horses have arrived," he said, taking his cue from her and trying to speak normally.

Rising from the log he assisted her to stand and they walked back together.

The way back took them through the stable yard, where Simpson was just parading Elvina's animals to the wide-eyed admiration of the stable hands.

The Duke stopped to regard the magnificent creatures with awe.

"Jupiter and Mars," Elvina told him proudly.

"Spirited names," the Duke commented. "Are they as spirited by nature?"

"I would not have them any other way!"

He walked around them, running his hands up and down their legs.

"I am jealous," he finally pronounced. "I have nothing so good in my stables."

He eyed her strangely.

"The mystery deepens," he murmured quietly.

And walked away.

Elvina followed him at a distance and rounded the corner of the house just as a very smart carriage was bowling up to the front door.

It was drawn by two matching white horses and driven by a liveried coachman. On the door a grand coat of arms was emblazoned.

In the back sat two elegantly dressed ladies, one middle-aged and one in her twenties. The face of the latter was petulant, but otherwise without character.

Elvina entered the house by a side door and hurried up to the library, where she found Violet leaning out of the window. Violet whirled when she saw her enter.

"Do you see who's here?" she asked in horror.

"I saw two ladies in a carriage. Who are they?"

"Lady Gorleston, widow of the Earl of Gorleston and her daughter, Lady Alexandra. And I hate them both."

"Violet, you must not say that."

"Why not? It's true, especially Lady Gorleston. She is a tiresome woman who never leaves David alone. She flatters him and makes up to him."

"I suppose everyone does, because he's a Duke."

"It's disgusting. He should not let her do it."

"How can he stop her? Besides, he must be so used to it, I doubt if he notices."

"I try to make up for it by being rude to her, but with him there I cannot be as rude as I want to be!"

"You must not be rude to her at all," Elvina advised. "The new Violet is charming, delightful and inspires everyone she meets."

Violet laughed.

"Is that what you expect me to be?" she asked.

"Of course. As your brother would say, you have a position to keep up."

"Do I have to be charming for *that*?" Violet asked, aghast.

Elvina could not help laughing at Violet's gloomy expression.

"I hate Lady Gorleston," she repeated. "She has been really nasty about me, not only to her friends and her family, but also to David.

"I think she wants David to marry Alexandra. And then she would contrive to move in here as well. She is a widow with no other daughters. But I cannot think of anything more ghastly than if she was running the house, doing me down, and I am quite certain making David unhappy."

Elvina stared at her as the implications of this image struck home. If the Duke married someone who was not understanding and kind to Violet, she would revert and be as difficult and unpleasant as she had been when Elvina arrived.

Almost as if Violet knew what Elvina was thinking, she said,

"She will certainly be very jealous of you. I have heard the servants say that she is jealous of everyone in the County who is young and pretty.

"She will get Alexandra to marry David so that she can come and rule the roost here."

"Is your brother attracted by Lady Alexandra?"

"No, of course not," Violet answered quickly. "But he has to marry and have an heir and it needs to be someone like her."

"Why?"

"I mean it has to be a woman with a title. She is an Earl's daughter. I suppose a Viscount's daughter would do, but he couldn't really go lower."

"And what about love?" Elvina demanded, horrified. "Is your brother so arrogant and lofty that he thinks love does not matter?"

"I am sure he would rather choose a wife he loved, but he knows he cannot have everything."

"And his wife's social position matters most, does it?" Violet stared at her.

"Well, he thinks it does. He cannot just please himself. He has to do his duty to the family. I know that is what he would say."

"And what do you say?"

Violet sighed ecstatically.

"I want to be just like *Romeo and Juliet*."

"They ended up dead," Elvina reminded her prosaically.

"I just mean that I want to follow my heart wherever it leads. And, of course, I want David to do the same. Lady Gorleston must not have her way."

"Violet, you keep saying Lady Gorleston, but it's her daughter he would be marrying. She may not want to."

"Not want to marry a Duke? Anyway, she will obey what her mother tells her."

"Then we have to save your brother and we have to save him very cleverly. If you simply attack her, as you have been doing, your brother may think he has to protect her."

Violet was listening intently as Elvina continued,

"You must be very charming, so that she doesn't look too good by contrast."

She was interrupted by the arrival of a footman.

"His Grace's compliments and he would like both Lady Violet and Mrs. Winters to join him for lunch, which will be in half an hour. Lady Gorleston and Lady Alexandra will be present."

"Are you quite sure that I am included?" Elvina wanted to know.

"His Grace was very particular about that point, ma'am."

"Thank you. Please tell His Grace that we will be there punctually."

As soon as he left Elvina urged,

"Hurry now. We must appear at our best."

She dressed Violet in a very pretty pink dress from her own wardrobe. Then she looked again through her clothes, wishing she had brought something plainer and more befitting a governess.

But the best she could find was a dark blue gown that despite its simplicity was full of elegance.

Violet was overjoyed to see her.

"She will certainly be furious that you look so nice and so smart," she commented, "and not at all like a governess."

"That's just what I don't want her to think," Elvina contradicted her. "I will just try to fade into the background and not rouse the suspicions of 'the danger' who is sitting downstairs."

"You are quite right to call her 'the danger'," Violet agreed. "I only hope we have enough weapons on our side."

"We have you and make no mistake you look very, very pretty," Elvina replied. "From what you have told me I am quite certain that will annoy her."

"It will infuriate her," Violet said gleefully.

"Now is the time to show your brother you are a very different person from the one you were before," Elvina told her. "Remember, however nasty these ladies may be to you, you have to be delightful as a contrast to them."

"And you will help me, you promise," Violet pleaded.

"Of course I will," Elvina said. "But I have to see them first and be quite certain they are as bad as you say. *After that the battle will begin*!"

They walked down the stairs together.

When they heard voices coming from the drawing room, Elvina's eyes twinkled as she looked at Violet.

"You look *so* lovely," she told her. "Remember our plan of campaign."

Violet drew in her breath.

"I am ready for anything," she whispered.

Elvina could not help laughing.

As they walked in Elvina saw that the Duke was standing by the window.

He was obviously pointing out something in the garden to the ladies who were standing beside him.

One look at Lady Gorleston told Elvina that she was a danger not only to Violet but also to the Duke. She was the type of female whom Elvina had met quite often in London.

Women who were anxious to make sure their daughters or perhaps their husbands were important because of the gain to themselves.

She was, perhaps, in her late forties, with a hard face that must once have been beautiful before arrogance and selfishness soured it.

Her daughter was a younger, more pallid version of herself. She looked weak and slightly foolish and equally ill-humoured.

As the Duke had heard the door open when Violet and Elvina entered, he turned round towards them and a pleased smile came over his face as he saw Violet.

The expressions of the two ladies froze.

Aware of the impression she was creating, Violet moved forward and held out her hand to Lady Gorleston.

"How lovely to see you," she smiled. "I thought it must be you when I saw your smart carriage coming up the drive."

She spoke in such a friendly way that Lady Gorleston and the Duke were both surprised. Lady Alexandra looked confused.

Almost as though he was aware of tension in the air, the Duke hurried to say,

"Lady Gorleston, Lady Alexandra, you must meet Mrs. Winters who is a new addition to the castle. She has made such a change for the better in Violet's life."

Lady Gorleston turned lofty eyes towards Elvina.

"And Mrs. Winters is – ?"

"I am Lady Violet's governess."

She could almost have laughed at the surprise and fury in Lady Gorleston's face. Clearly she was not used to sitting down to lunch with governesses. Nor was this very smart and fashionable woman standing in front of her how she expected a governess to look.

Elvina had held out her hand, but Lady Gorleston ignored it. In fact she stared at her aggressively and angrily.

"How do you do," she said at last in a hard voice.

"How do you do, my Lady," Elvina said politely.

"My daughter, *Lady* Alexandra Gorleston. My love, this is Mrs. Winters. *The governess.*"

"How do you do, Lady Alexandra."

Lady Alexandra inclined her head and murmured something, but plainly she would do nothing until she knew which way her mother would turn.

In a cold hard voice Lady Gorleston asked,

"Am I to understand that you are *employed* to teach this poor child, who has been unlucky up to now in those who have been *hired* for this purpose?"

"I am very fortunate to be here in this lovely castle," Elvina replied. "Violet has shown me the horses, which as I am sure you appreciate, are wonderful. They would be the envy of every rider in the South."

Lady Gorleston turned almost rudely towards the Duke to comment,

"You must be glad that after so many difficulties, you have at last found someone who will instruct poor Violet in everything essential before she makes her debut."

There was silence.

Then Elvina said,

"It isn't commonly known that Lady Violet is extremely accomplished. She could read before she was four years old and she is reading her way right through the magnificent Castleforde library."

Because she spoke so admiringly, the Duke smiled at her and remarked,

"I think the truth is that few people enjoy the library as much as you do, Mrs. Winters."

As he spoke, Elvina was aware that Lady Gorleston stiffened.

There was fury in her eyes, but for the moment she could not think of anything to say.

Then, before the Duke could reply, the butler came in to announce,

"Luncheon is served, Your Grace," and all heads turned towards him.

"Good!" the Duke exclaimed. He gave Lady Gorleston an engaging smile and offered her his arm.

"Why don't you take Alexandra in?" she asked immediately. "Alexandra, my dear, take the Duke's arm."

Smiling like a well-behaved doll, the girl did so. He accepted the change graciously and led her into the dining room.

Before following them Lady Gorleston turned back to Elvina and said with lofty graciousness,

"So delightful to meet you Mrs. Winters. Such a shame that we have to part so soon."

"But we are not parting, my Lady," Elvina replied. "I am coming in to lunch."

Lady Gorleston's face was a study of horror.

"You? A governess?"

"His Grace has been kind enough to invite me," Elvina parried, refusing to be discomposed by the other woman's icy glare.

"In that case," Lady Gorleston said in a hard voice, "I suppose you had better come."

Turning, she stormed into the dining room, leaving Elvina and Violet to exchange significant glances.

CHAPTER SEVEN

The table that had been laid for them was round and just large enough for five people, a welcome change from the huge oblong table where the Duke normally dined.

The Duke seated Lady Alexandra on his right and her mother on his left. Lady Gorleston shoved her way in front of Elvina, as though afraid that she might take a better seat than was a servant's right.

But Elvina had the last laugh, because she found herself sitting directly opposite the Duke.

Violet turned the conversation to horses. It might have been innocently done, but the three of them knew all about horses and it soon became obvious that the Gorleston ladies knew very little.

Good manners kept Elvina from pressing a subject which would show the guests at a disadvantage, but when Violet mentioned breeding it was too much for her.

"David is as good as any breeder you have ever known, isn't he Mrs. Winters?" Violet enquired provocatively.

"I am certain of it. Your Grace, it would be a tremendous success for the County, as well as yourself, if you challenged some of the other breeders who, I can assure you, are not as good as you are."

She sensed Lady Gorleston stiffen. Since when did governesses assure their employers of something so far outside their duties?

Firmly she claimed his attention to say,

"My dear Duke, you are ignoring me and I wanted to ask you to come to Gorleston Towers next week. I plan to give a party in honour of your birthday."

"My birthday?" he exclaimed in surprise. "But it's not – good Heavens, so it is! I shall be thirty-four."

"And we must mark such an important occasion suitably," Lady Gorleston cooed. "Mustn't we, Alexandra?"

"Yes, Mama."

"Dear girl, she's so enthusiastic! On the way here she kept asking if I thought you would be pleased. 'My love', I told her, 'when the Duke knows that you are putting yourself out to celebrate his birthday, he will be delighted.' And then she was ecstatic."

There was a stunned moment, during which the others contemplated Lady Alexandra being ecstatic.

"You were overwhelmed with joy, were you not, my dear?"

"Yes, Mama."

"This is most kind," the Duke said in a carefully expressionless voice, "but I beg you not go to any trouble – "

"But it is no trouble at all," Lady Gorleston gushed. "You must come and stay the night at Gorleston Towers. And Violet, of course, must come with you. A small party will be the perfect preparation for her debut next year."

"Oh, yes!" Violet agreed. Then, turning to Elvina, she sighed, "won't that be exciting?" "There will, of course, be no need for Mrs. Winters to come," Lady Gorleston added.

After a small silence, the Duke said,

"Mrs. Winters is as much a friend as a governess, and I prefer Violet not to go anywhere except under her chaperonage."

But Lady Gorleston was not ready to give up.

"Oh, but dear Violet will be under my care and I shall personally ensure that she will looked after perfectly."

"I am sure that you will do so admirably, Countess, but I prefer Violet to remain in the care of her friend.

"It is kind of you to want to mark my birthday, but I think it would be better if I held a small celebration here. Then your whole family could come and Violet can learn Society behaviour in her own home."

Thoroughly outmanoeuvred, Lady Gorleston had no choice but to smile and assure him mendaciously of her delight.

Gleefully aware of these undercurrents, Violet burst out with,

"And you must tell us where I can buy some pretty dresses? Mrs. Winters is horrified at how out-of-date and old-fashioned my wardrobe is. We want to go shopping to buy me some beautiful clothes, like she herself owns."

After what had just been said, Lady Gorleston was so infuriated that Elvina almost burst out laughing at the expression in her eyes.

Before she could say anything the Duke chipped in, "That *is* a good idea. I am sure Mrs. Winters has a marvellous taste in clothes as she herself is always so smart. But I doubt if the shops in our nearest town sell the kind of fashions that she bought in London."

"Perhaps her Ladyship can inform us of a good seamstress," suggested Elvina.

Fighting to recover lost ground, the Countess purred, "Of course I will help you in every way I can. I am sure if your sister needs a seamstress I will be able to find one."

"That is very thoughtful of you," the Duke said.

She gazed at him, placing her hand firmly on his arm.

"You know, dear David, I would do anything to help you."

The way she spoke and the caressing movement of her hand made Elvina well aware that what Violet had told her was the truth.

This woman, whom she had disliked as soon as she saw her, was after the Duke for her daughter as a way of moving into the castle herself.

Elvina was quite certain that she would do everything in her power to succeed.

'I must put a stop to her for Violet's sake,' she thought.

Then it flashed through her mind that perhaps she had another reason – to prevent this pushy, rather unpleasant woman from gaining what she desired. A personal reason.

But that was impossible, she thought. She was still in love with Andrew.

But Andrew's face was suddenly very blurred in her memory. Somehow the Duke's face seemed to be there instead.

As the meal was drawing to a close the Duke said,

"I think the best thing we can do is to listen to some music. I am sure our guests would enjoy hearing Violet play the piano, so we will go to the music room."

"There is no hurry," Lady Gorleston intervened. "If you wish for the ladies to leave you alone, as is correct, we will leave you to smoke a cigar before you join us."

"I can hardly smoke and drink alone, so I would rather come with you."

Defeated, Lady Gorleston swept into the music room.

Violet opened up the piano.

"You play first," she murmured to Elvina, "because you play better than me."

"Why don't you go and sit beside your brother while I play?" Elvina whispered, "and I will do so when you are at the piano."

Violet giggled softly.

"The old trout is furious and I am enjoying it more than I can tell you. You do see what a nasty, beastly woman she is."

"I agree with you that she is very unpleasant!"

At that moment the Duke had pulled a comfortable armchair in front of the platform.

As they sat down in the front seats, Violet jumped down from the platform and sat on the other side of her brother.

"Mrs. Winters plays so well," she sighed, "and I am determined to be as good as she is. Then you will be very proud of me."

As Elvina started to play, the Duke became aware of how badly he had needed this scenario. To sit here watching her, looking so beautiful and elegant and listening to the exquisite sounds that she was causing to flow from the piano, seemed to make a beautiful peace steal over him.

Suddenly he was pervaded by happiness that he only half understood.

Elvina played for over a quarter-of-an-hour before finishing triumphantly. The Duke applauded and exclaimed,

"That was wonderful! Absolutely wonderful! I had no idea that you could play so well."

"I am not always so fortunate to be able to play such a lovely piano," Elvina said. "And thank you for those kind words."

The Duke smiled at her.

She smiled back and it was as though everyone else in the room had vanished. Now she knew how badly she had missed him while he had been away.

And why.

The knowledge was overwhelming.

Lady Gorleston hung on until the last possible moment, but eventually even she was forced to concede defeat. After making many protestations of eagerness for the coming party, she departed with her daughter.

"A party, a party!" Violet cried excitedly. "I am so looking forward to it.

"We had better start sending out the invitations," the Duke suggested. "Mrs. Winters, I rely on you to help me with the organisation."

They talked about the party over dinner that evening.

Before they retired to bed the Duke said,

"I shall go out riding early tomorrow, if anyone wants to join me."

"Oh, yes," Elvina agreed. "Let us get up really early for a long ride before breakfast. To me it is always the best part of the day."

"I hoped you would come, because now I shall have the chance to see you ride one of your horses. Which will it be, I wonder?"

"I haven't yet made up my mind," Elvina teased.

He turned to his sister,

"I was very pleased to see that you made an effort to be polite to Lady Gorleston. Well done, my dear!"

"Thank you, thank you, darling David. I will try always to make you proud of me."

She hugged and kissed him.

Then she turned towards the stairs. Elvina held up her hand to say goodnight. As the Duke took it he asked,

"How is it possible you can have waved a magic wand and improved my sister so much? Everything that is happening now is so different from when you arrived that I think you must have come from Heaven!"

"That is what I want you to believe," Elvina replied. "Thank you for saying such kind things to me."

Holding her hand in both of his, the Duke looked at her.

For a moment as their eyes met, neither of them moved.

Then the same sweet sensation as before came over her. She murmured quickly,

"Thank you and goodnight."

She took her hand away as she spoke and ran down the corridor to follow Violet.

As she reached the staircase she wanted to look back to see if the Duke was still watching her. But she told herself that would be a mistake and skipped up the stairs to where Violet was waiting.

As they walked to their own rooms, Violet called out,

"I am so looking forward to tomorrow."

"So am I," Elvina said absently. "Goodnight, my dear."

Then she went to her own room. Quickly she undressed and climbed into bed.

She lay very still for a long time, looking into the darkness and wondering what was happening to her.

*

When she woke early in the morning she felt suddenly excited at the thought of riding again with the Duke.

She jumped out of bed and ran to Violet's room. She found she was already awake and drawing back the curtains.

"I have been thinking about David's birthday and what to buy him for a gift," she said. "After all, he has everything."

"There is one thing he does not have, which surprises me," Elvina suggested. "Most men seem to have a dog in the country, but he doesn't have one."

"That is because David's dog died when he was quite young," Violet explained. "He was broken-hearted and never owned a dog again. But I am sure, although he has never said so, that he misses having one."

"Of course he does," Elvina agreed. "Every man likes a dog. What sort of dog was it?"

"A Labrador," Violet replied.

"Then that is what we should give him for his birthday," Elvina stated firmly.

"There's a man in a village, not far from here, who breeds Labradors."

"We must go and see him as soon as possible."

They ate breakfast quickly, then ran to the stables and found the Duke already there.

"You are late," he said jokingly. "Mrs. Winters you are riding Jupiter this morning. Simpson says so."

"Oh, well, if Simpson says so, then I must."

At that moment Simpson appeared leading Jupiter. When Elvina had greeted him he said, "Mars is a little unsettled after the journey, ma'am, and he only needs gentle exercise for the moment."

"And how do you know that I am not planning to take gentle exercise this morning?" she asked, raising her voice so that he could hear.

Simpson grinned.

"I don't think so, ma'am."

"No, I don't either," the Duke agreed, also grinning.

"I'll ride Mars myself, ma'am."

"I don't think I will need you this morning, Simpson."

"I think you will, ma'am," he countered firmly.

As soon as they were out of the yard they all gave their horses their heads, so that Elvina and the Duke outstripped Violet. Soon she was far behind, but with Simpson looking after her, they knew there was no need for them to be concerned.

When they neared the stream, the Duke pulled in his mount.

"I cannot beat your wonderful horse," he declared. "I can only just keep up with him. I will pay you anything you want for him."

Elvina merely laughed.

"You won't sell him to me?"

"Did you really think I would?"

"No, not for a moment."

As their horses drank from the stream the Duke said,

"I am looking forward to hearing you play again tonight. I have been thinking about it ever since we said goodnight yesterday evening."

"Yes," she agreed. "After I had played last night, I felt the melody inside me and I was accompanied by it all night. I woke up with it still singing in my head."

She spoke in a dreamy way which made the Duke look at her.

"I thought when I was listening to you last night," he said, "that you were thinking about love. It certainly seemed to come out to us from your fingers."

"I only hope that is true," Elvina sighed.

"I think some people are musical even when they are just thinking, but you gave us music last night which seemed to come from your heart."

"It did come from my heart, because I was thanking the angels who brought me here."

She spoke with utter sincerity. Then as her eyes met the Duke's, they both felt there was no need for them to say any more. For a moment there was silence.

"Hey!"

They both turned to find that Violet was catching up with them with Simpson in the rear.

"Let's race each other," she cried, setting off as she spoke.

It seemed as if the Duke could not take his eyes off Elvina. Then he seemed to wake up.

"We should go," he said.

Then they were all three racing each other to the end of the field. The Duke won by a neck.

Laughing together they rode home.

Elvina felt somehow that they had spent a happier morning than she had enjoyed for a very long time.

Something was happening between herself and the Duke, but there were no words to describe it.

It was better that way. Words could spoil everything.

The three of them ate a cheerful lunch together before the Duke left for a meeting with the Lord Lieutenant of the County.

"What are the two of you going to do this afternoon?" he asked as he prepared for departure.

"Oh, – this and that," Violet replied airily.

He raised his eyebrows in Elvina's direction.

"This and that," she repeated, smiling back at him mysteriously.

"Then I will leave the two of you to your secrets."

As soon as he had gone Violet giggled,

"Now he's wondering. This is going to be such fun."

"Give him time to leave properly," Elvina said. "And then we'll go."

They took the carriage into the nearby village and after enquiring the way, managed to find the house where the puppy breeder lived.

When they drew up outside the front door, they could already hear high pitched yelps coming from inside.

Instead of knocking at the front door they wandered around the back where there was a large garden. They stopped in delight at the sight that awaited them.

In the centre of the lawn was a black Labrador and gambolling round her were three black puppies, two large and one tiny. From the way she occasionally nuzzled them, especially the tiny one, it was clear that they were her offspring.

"Can I help you ladies?" asked a man, dressed in working clothes, who was filling a bowl with feed.

"I think we have already found what we are looking for," Elvina replied. "Are they for sale?"

"The two large ones are," the man said. "We're keeping the little one because he's his mother's favourite. The other two are the naughtiest pups you ever knew!"

"Good. They are the ones we want," Elvina exclaimed. "The naughtier the better."

The deal was soon settled. The pups were expensive, but Elvina paid the price without protest, knowing by instinct that these two bundles of mischief would suit the Duke better than any others.

As they drove home Violet commented,

"I did not realise that it would be so much. I will pay you back, but I don't have much of my allowance left at the moment."

"It doesn't matter."

"Oh, but it does. I must buy them or they won't be my gift."

"Buy one. Let me give him the other."

"All right. That will be nice. Oh, David's going to be so thrilled. I wonder what names we should give them."

"We must leave that to him," Elvina replied. "It has always annoyed me when someone has given me an animal that already had a name. Then I have to keep the name whether I like it or not, so as not to confuse the poor creature."

"David will love them," Violet said in delight. "He cried when he lost Bruno, his last dog, although he did not let anyone see the tears in his eyes."

'No, he would not have done,' Elvina thought. 'He had been reared to be serious and had inherited his responsibilities too soon. There had been too few people in his life to whom he could feel close. He loved his sister, but she was too young to be his confidante. Perhaps his beloved dog was the only creature he could trust.

'And then Bruno had died, leaving him terribly alone, with no one to turn to. And he had closed in on himself. His duty to his great house had become all important and he had almost forgotten how vital it was to love.'

"Bruno's death must have made him very lonely," she reflected. "And very vulnerable."

"Yes," Violet agreed hotly. "Vulnerable to scheming women and their matchmaking Mamas."

"That is why you must protect him by becoming closer to him," Elvina advised. "So that he doesn't end up marrying the wrong woman out of loneliness."

"I wonder what the right woman would be like," Violet mused.

'*Yes, I wonder,*' Elvina thought, although she did not say it aloud. '*Is she anything like me?*' "Well, if he marries Alexandra I shall run away," Violet declared mutinously.

"You will not run away," Elvina said. "You are going to stay and make your brother happy until someone tall, attractive, charming and very intelligent asks you to marry him."

Violet burst out laughing,

"Do you *really* think that will really happen to me?"

"Of course it will," Elvina told her. "You have to be very careful and quite certain that a man marries you because you are you and not for what you possess."

There was silence for a moment. Then Violet asked,

"How do you know when a man is really in love with you and not just entranced because you have money and a title?"

It was a question which Elvina had often asked herself. After a while she responded,

"I think you would have to trust your heart to tell you."

"But would your heart always know?"

"Yes," Elvina murmured. "If it was real, you would know everything, because he would be a man incapable of falsehood."

As she spoke she knew that Andrew had vanished from her heart entirely and had been replaced by the Duke.

Instinct told her that he was truly incapable of falsehood and if he ever told her that he loved her, it would be the truth.

If he ever told her.

*

As they arrived home Violet queried,

"Where are we going to keep the puppies? I suppose we ought to put them in the stables."

She did not sound very keen and Elvina immediately suggested,

"I think we should keep them with us for safety. Let's take them up to my room."

Having sworn the coachman to secrecy, they crept up the back stairs until they reached Elvina's room and darted inside.

"We have to be organised," Elvina said. "We need food from the kitchen and some newspaper."

"I can fetch newspapers from the library," Violet volunteered.

"Good. You do that while I find them somewhere to sleep."

She solved the problem by emptying a drawer, placing it on the floor and lining it with one of her own dresses.

"I never much liked that dress," she told the pups, who were eyeing her with interest. "Now it's all yours!"

Violet dashed in, eyes brimming with fun.

"I have brought all the newspapers from the library. But David came in and found me and said had I suddenly developed an interest in current affairs? I told him I was fascinated by politics and it was all your doing."

"You terrible girl!" Elvina exclaimed. "What have you let me in for?"

They found out over dinner. The Duke was in a good humour and teased them both about Violet's new found interest in serious matters. Elvina teased him back, until at last he admitted, grinning,

"I can see I am going to learn nothing. All right, keep your secrets!"

At that moment there was the faint but unmistakable sound of a yap.

Elvina and Violet stiffened, looking at each other, aghast. The Duke seemed untroubled. Either he had not heard the yap or it did not strike him as odd.

"How did your meeting go?" Violet asked.

He began to talk about the Lord Lieutenant, breaking off to take a sip of wine.

Yap!

This time he heard it.

"What was that?" he asked, frowning.

"Nothing," they said together.

"I could have sworn I heard – "

Yap!

110

The Duke looked around. Six footmen in livery and powdered wigs lined the walls, three to a side.

"Did any of you hear anything?"

One by one the footmen said, "no, Your Grace," until only one man was left.

"What about you, Willis?" the Duke asked.

It was one of his talents that made him loved among his staff that he knew each one of them by name. All two hundred of them.

"Willis?" the Duke said again. "Is something wrong."

Willis, a huge, dignified individual gave his employer a painful look and forced himself to say,

"A small creature is disgracing himself on my foot, Your Grace."

CHAPTER EIGHT

How the Duke laughed! Elvina and Violet threw up their hands and then buried their faces in them, horrified but laughing too.

Next Elvina hurried across the floor to seize the miscreant who had by now finished his work and settled contentedly in her arms.

Violet was regarding her brother with relief.

"You're not angry?" she asked.

"How can I be angry? I don't know when I have enjoyed anything so much. I thought nothing could bring Willis's dignity down."

His voice became gentler as he laid a hand on the footman's shoulder.

"Forgive me. You had better take the rest of the evening off."

"Thank you, Your Grace!" the footman said, immediately forgiving the Duke for his laughter.

"What a splendid little fellow!" the Duke exclaimed, regarding the pup. "Where does he come from? Is he yours, Violet?"

"No, he is *yours*," she cried. "Oh, dear! Now the surprise is spoiled."

"Surprise?"

"This is your birthday present."

"This?" A look of fond pleasure broke over the Duke's face. "He is your present to me?"

"Mrs. Winters said you looked lonely without a dog – "

"Violet, I didn't exactly say – "

"Well, anyway, he's yours," Violet repeated hastily.

"Happy birthday – a week early."

Elvina held the pup out and the Duke took him gently from her hands.

"Thank you," he said. "It was a lovely thought. I shall call him Blackie."

"But the other one is black as well," Violet protested.

"Yes, we bought two," Elvina explained. "We couldn't resist them. We were going to hide them upstairs."

"For a week?"

"Yes, it wasn't very practical, was it? I wonder how he got out. And where is his brother? We hid them in my room. The maid must have gone in and left the door open."

"Do you mean there might be another one wandering around the castle?" the Duke asked.

"We had better find out," Elvina urged.

The three of them hurried out of the dining room and up the stairs.

When they reached her bedroom door, Elvina said breathlessly,

"Cross your fingers!" Then she opened the door.

The room was very silent and she was suddenly filled with foreboding.

"Is anything wrong, Your Grace?"

A maid had appeared in the corridor and was looking at them all in surprise.

"Do you know who's been in here recently?" Elvina asked.

"Yes, miss, I have. I brought you some fresh linen."

"They must have sneaked out then," Elvina said. "I don't think the other one's here. How long ago were you in this room?"

"About an hour ago, miss."

"He could be anywhere by now," Violet groaned.

"Then we had better start looking," the Duke said.

"Did I do wrong, Your Grace?" the maid asked worriedly.

"Not at all," he told her kindly. "But please pass the word all around the castle. If anyone sees a black puppy, he belongs to me."

Violet, who knew her brother better than anyone, was regarding him curiously.

"We had better call him by name," the Duke suggested.

"He doesn't have a name," Elvina pointed out.

"We'll call him Blackie."

"But you are holding Blackie," Violet objected.

"It's no use, he will just have to be called Blackie as well. We need some name to call him."

Elvina and Violet looked at each other, considering how to explain to him that he was being illogical. But it would have been useless. A new light had come on inside the Duke and he seemed strangely happy.

"We must each take a different direction," he said. "I will go along this corridor, Violet, you go in the other direction and Mrs. Winters, you head for that staircase."

They set off, each of them calling, *"Blackie! Blackie!"* loudly.

Elvina headed for the staircase the Duke had indicated.

It led to the rear of the castle and descended to the kitchens. She ran all the way down to the ground floor and stood listening, for she could sense something.

"Your Grace," she called, returning half way up the staircase, "I think he may be here, but it's too dark to see."

From above she heard him say,

"Violet, are you there? Here, take Blackie before he disgraces himself again."

A moment later he was beside Elvina, only half visible in the gloom.

"There's a noise coming from down there."

From down below came a faint scratching noise.

"Blackie!" the Duke called.

Yap!

"He's under the stairs."

Elvina made her way down gingerly, calling, "Blackie!"

This time, instead of the yap there came a pitiful whine.

"Poor little thing, you are lost and frightened," she muttered. "You shouldn't have run away."

There was a small table by the wall and she knelt down beside it, guided by the whining. But when she reached out the pup scuttled away.

"Don't run away from me," she begged.

"I've got him," came the Duke's voice from where he was kneeling at the other end of the table. "No, I haven't. Hey, come here!"

The puppy, a small black shadow in the semi-darkness, slithered away. They both lunged for him at the same moment.

Then something seemed to thump Elvina and the next moment she felt the floor beneath her back.

115

"Mrs. Winters," he enquired sharply. "Are you all right?"

"Yes, I – I seem to have slipped."

"We collided and I knocked you over. I am so sorry. Let me help you up."

She felt his hands on her shoulders, drawing her upright. Instinctively she clung to him to steady herself.

And then there was silence and stillness. Something seemed to transfix them both.

In the gloom she could hear him breathing and feel the warmth of his breath on her face. That warmth seemed to be pervading her whole body, streaming through every part of her.

Suddenly the moment was full of blazing excitement and she could hear the thunder of her own heartbeat.

The next instant she felt his lips on hers and his arms about her. Instinctively she pressed against him, responding with her whole heart, knowing that this was what she wanted, what she had always secretly desired.

"Mrs. Winters – " he murmured.

Never had words sounded so beautiful.

"Forgive me," he said. "I know I have no right – "

But then his arms tightened again and he was kissing her more passionately than ever. This time Elvina put her own arms around his neck, filled with delight at the feel of his lips and the sense of his heart beating against hers.

She could feel him trembling, but at the same time his body was tense, as though he was engaged in some overwhelming inner struggle.

She knew then that he had kissed her against his will and that he should break free if only he could.

But she would not let him.

She moved her lips gently against his, trying to tell him silently that he must not break free. She desperately wanted this heavenly moment to last forever.

But then the spell was broken, not by him, but by a voice that echoed down the stairs.

"Hallo, is anybody down there?"

It was Violet calling to them.

Hastily they pulled apart, but for a moment neither could summon the strength to stand up. They knelt where they were, on the floor, neither quite sure what had happened, but each trying to come to terms with what they could not understand.

At last the Duke rose to his feet and helped her to stand up. Elvina could feel that he was still trembling.

"Bl-Blackie," she stammered in a shaking voice. "Where is he?"

"He managed to slither away between us," the Duke mumbled and his voice too was shaking.

"Are you there?" Violet called again.

She was coming nearer. They moved apart and turned away, both feeling confused and distracted.

"Have you found him?" Violet asked, reaching the bottom step. She was still holding the first puppy.

"No," Elvina answered vaguely. "He rushed away – he may not have been here – "

"But he's over there," Violet said, pointing to a corner.

And there he was, crouched in the corner, looking worried and squeaking.

"Poor little thing," Elvina muttered.

"He'll be all right," the Duke said, reaching down. "He was just worried in case his Master didn't come for him. But here I am and now he has nothing to worry about."

"Perhaps I should fetch a lamp," Violet offered.

"No need," her brother told her. "I've got him. Come along, little fellow. No more escaping."

They made their way back upstairs to where the corridors were well lit.

"Let me see them both," the Duke asked.

Violet held up the pup she was holding and the Duke looked from one to the other.

"They are exactly alike," he said chuckling. "Blackie and Blackie."

"David, you're surely not going to give them the same name?"

"Why not? They know who they are now. Let's not confuse them!"

Violet began to giggle and they all laughed.

The Duke took the second pup and held them both, one tucked under each arm. It was a delightful sight and later Elvina remembered it as one of her happiest moments.

By now the servants had also become aware that His Grace was behaving in an incredible fashion and were appearing through doorways and up the stairs, all wanting to share in the excitement.

When he realised that he had an audience he turned and grinned at them all.

"Here they are everyone," he called. "The new members of the household. "Come and see."

They all crowded around to look at the pups. Some of them cast nervous looks at the Duke, as if wondering at the change in him and how long it would last.

But at last they dared to reach out and touch each of the little black bundles.

"Have you named them, Your Grace?" one of the maids asked, which drew her a look of reproof from Pearson, the butler, for normally only he was permitted to address the Duke directly.

"Yes," the Duke answered her. "I have named them Blackie and Blackie. It will save calling for them separately."

"But they'll both come, Your Grace," the housekeeper pointed out.

"Excellent. Since they will live together and with me at all times, that will be the best arrangement."

He looked so genial that everyone broke into smiles. Nobody had ever seen His Grace so at ease before. It was as though a glow of benevolence had taken over the whole castle.

"I think we should spend a little time in the library getting to know them," the Duke proposed. "Pearson, perhaps you would be so good as to arrange some suitable refreshment." "Very good, Your Grace. Would wine and cakes be acceptable?"

"I meant for the dogs."

"Certainly, Your Grace," he said stiffly.

"Wine and cakes will do nicely for us," the Duke agreed, relenting. "I suggest you try the stables for the rest. I know my head groom keeps a dog."

The three of them spent the next two hours very happily in the library, laughing over the antics of the two Blackies.

119

The puppies learned their names quickly and in a short time they would bound across the floor together when their new Master called them, already seeming to race each other for the honour of getting there first.

He dealt with them kindly, distributing titbits with strict fairness.

"I am glad to see you don't favour one over the other," Elvina remarked.

"Considering I cannot tell them apart, that would be very difficult," he said with a smile.

But then he grew serious and added,

"Having favourites is something I would never permit. It is cruel. It can break a child's heart."

"But these are dogs," she said.

He gave an awkward laugh.

"Yes, of course, but – the truth is that I suffered badly as a child. I had a brother, a year younger than myself.

"He was my mother's darling and my father's too, although he was not a man given to warm feelings. Such love as he had to give went to my brother. When they looked at Simon their faces would soften and their eyes were full of joy. That never happened with me.

"Of course, as the eldest and the heir, I received a great deal of attention. But that was family duty and I knew the difference, because family duty was drummed into me from the very first moment. A Castleforde did this. A Castleforde did not do that. The rules were strict and never to be broken.

"I had a whole army of tutors and companions to make sure I knew what was expected of me. But it was never the same as being loved."

Even now, all these years later, his voice was wistful, as though somewhere inside him there still lived that lonely boy, wondering desolately why he could not inspire love.

Elvina's heart ached for him and perhaps something of that feeling showed in her voice, for when she said, "how sad!" he looked up at her quickly with a grateful smile.

"I promised myself that it is something I would never do to anyone else," he said.

"It's strange that Violet has never spoken about her other brother."

"He died when she was three years old and he had joined the Army by that time, so he was never at home. She knows that he once existed, but he was never very real to her.

"My parents did not survive long after that and I am sure that losing him hastened their deaths. The odd part is that Simon and I were on good terms. I was jealous of him, but also fond of him and apart from some of the older servants I am probably the only person left who remembers him."

Another creature lost to him, Elvina thought. How lonely and unloving his life had been!

And it showed itself in consideration for the feelings of a small defenceless dog. She regarded him fondly, while both puppies greedily accepted morsels of food from his hands oblivious of all else.

She wondered if he would mention the kiss they had shared in the shadows. But she guessed that he would say nothing while Violet was in the room, even though she was at the other end. This was a moment for warmth and friendship, not passion.

Then she saw the glow in his eyes and knew that the passion was still there, even while he concealed it for the sake of propriety.

"You once said that you like to ride early," he reminded her, "before the rest of the household is awake."

"Oh, yes, that is the best time."

"I think so too," he murmured. "Hey, Violet, this dog's eating all my cake."

They drank wine and fed most of the cakes to Blackie and Blackie as titbits. Then Elvina noticed Violet scribbling some figures at the table.

"I am working out how I am going to pay you for the puppies," she admitted when Elvina asked.

"There is no need."

"But of course there is. If I don't pay you, they will be your gift."

"What are you two talking about?" the Duke enquired, coming to the table.

"Can I have advance on my allowance?" Violet asked him. "I owe Mrs. Winters for a puppy."

"I would much rather make both of them my gift," Elvina said.

"I would appreciate that," the Duke intervened unexpectedly. "If it's not more than you can afford?"

"It's not and I would be glad to give them both to you," she assured him.

"Leave it at that, then. Perhaps Violet can think of something else?"

"I will still need an advance on my allowance," Violet insisted.

It was on the tip of her tongue to ask why Mrs. Winters should want to give him both dogs, or why he should want that. But then she looked from one to the other and something held her silent.

In many ways Violet was a perceptive young lady.

*

Elvina was out with the dawn next morning, galloping over the fields on Mars, but always able to keep the castle in view. At last she looked back and saw the Duke pursuing her on Jupiter.

"I took your consent for granted," he said, catching up with her.

"I am sure Simpson had something to say about that," she chuckled.

"He tried, but I did what *he* always does – became deaf."

She roared with laughter and the Duke joined in. The next moment they had urged their horses forward and were flying across the ground together.

They galloped until they had shaken the fidgets out of the animals' legs and slowed down near a stream. Dismounting they led the horses to water and watched them drink.

"I thought of you all night," he began.

She did not try to answer in words, but smiled and nodded her head.

"But if I tell you what I was thinking," he continued, "you might not believe me."

She raised her eyebrows.

"Then you can surprise me."

"I was remembering our talk. Our kiss was beautiful, but it was what I told you that stayed in my mind. I have never spoken about myself as I did to you."

"You don't talk about your feelings easily, do you?" she asked softly.

"No, I never have done. There has never been anyone to tell. I could not confide in my parents and Violet is too young. The only one I could talk to was Bruno, but dogs have such short lives.

"When he died it hurt so much that I swore I would never have another one, even if it meant nobody to talk to. And then I found myself telling you about Simon, saying things I have never told anyone. And now I have the Blackies that you have given me."

"One of them was meant to be from Violet."

"No, I want them both to be from you without involving anyone else. Do you understand why?"

He was looking directly into her face and she looked back into his.

"Yes, I think I understand."

"I felt so close to you and that means more than anything in the world, more than – *oh, my dear!*"

On the last words his control broke and he pulled her into his arms, kissing her again and again.

"I was thinking of this too," he muttered hoarsely.

"So was I," she whispered against his lips.

Then there was no more words, no more thought, only the feel of his heart beating against hers, his mouth sweetly enticing hers into a world of delight.

"I promised myself that this would *not* happen," he said at last. "I made so many good resolutions, but – I am a selfish man. When I want something, I am afraid – "

Elvina laughed joyously. As long as she was the one he wanted, he could be as selfish as he liked!

"Can you forgive me?" he asked.

"For what?" she asked. "For wanting me?"

"For abusing your trust while you lived in my house under my protection, something that no gentleman would ever – oh, what am I saying?"

"I think you are telling me that the Duke is not a gentleman," she laughed.

"I suppose I am. But I regret nothing if only you forgive me."

"Anything, anything," she said fervently.

"I should never – never – "

His words faltered and she saw the ardent look come back into his eyes. The next moment he was kissing her again and she was revelling in it.

Then they were laughing together, as though at some private joke that only they understood.

They headed their horses out over the fields, riding side by side towards the rising sun.

In her delirium of joy it never occurred to Elvina that there was something ominous about his words.

Yet afterwards she realised that she ought to have seen it. For he had already placed all the clues in her hands.

*

The next week was passed in an orgy of organisation. The three of them drew up lists of guests and Violet sent out the invitations with Elvina's help.

Somehow the Duke always found an excuse to join them in the library with his two new companions.

"I do not intend this to be a very large party," he declared. "About thirty, perhaps."

"You will have to invite far more than that or risk offending people," Violet advised him.

In the event they settled on fifty. When all the invitations had been despatched, there was the serious business of deciding what to wear.

Naturally Violet must have a new dress and a seamstress came to the castle to make her a beautiful creation of pink silk gauze.

Elvina would also have liked a new gown, but she decided to dress quietly. There would be time enough for her to relish dressing up in high fashion when her relationship with the Duke was out in the open.

That would be soon enough, she supposed. She knew that he loved her. He made it plain in a thousand ways.

Late at night, when Violet had gone to bed, he would join her in the library and they would talk.

He told her about the castle, about his family. Sometimes he spoke about himself as he had done when he told her about his dead brother.

All the time Elvina enjoyed a marvellous feeling of growing closer to him and of being able to see straight into his mind, because he was revealing himself to her.

Later she was to wonder how she could have been so stupid.

As the day of the party grew near the castle was seized by a frenzy of excitement. Everywhere was cleaned and polished until it shone. The dining table was extended to its fullest. When the evening finally arrived, Violet's maid dressed her carefully under Elvina's supervision. When she had finished she looked a dream in pink gauze with the Castleforde pearls adorning her neck.

Elvina wore pale grey satin with an opal necklace and tiny opal ear-rings.

She looked out of the window at the view over the grounds now bathed in a golden glow as the sun began to set. Just below she could see the Duke strolling on the terrace, the puppies at his heels, as they never left his side.

She felt a sudden desire for a few moments with him. The guests would be arriving soon, so she would have to be quick.

Running down the stairs she was just in time to see him come in from the terrace and head for the library. In another moment she had darted into the room with him, closing the door.

He turned, smiling with pleasure at the sight of her.

"How pretty you are," he said. "You will outshine every woman tonight."

"I do hope not," she smiled. "Think how furious the Gorlestons would be."

To her surprise a cloud came over his face.

"Yes. The Gorlestons. How I wish I could forget them! Oh, my darling, if you knew how hard I have tried to believe that none of it matters."

"None of what matters?" she asked, puzzled.

"Doing what is suitable," he replied with a touch of bitterness. "The pride of my house. How I have fought to convince myself that it was something I could set aside because of my love for you."

His face was ravaged, tormented, as he continued,

"But – but – *I cannot.* I was raised to put certain principles above all others and I cannot change."

The first faint chill began to pass over her heart, but she quelled it, looking searchingly into his face. What she suspected could not be true.

"My darling," he sighed heavily, "can you ever forgive me for the unpardonable liberties I have taken, knowing that I can never marry you?"

"What?" she cried, aghast. "Liberties? You have called me your dearest and I have called you *my* dearest."

"And you *are* my dearest. Dearer to me than anyone has ever been."

"And you talk about taking liberties as though I were some servant girl – "

"No, no, of course not," he said hurriedly. "You are no servant, but a gentlewoman, I have always recognised that. But I – "

He stopped and there was a long agonised pause.

"But what?" she asked.

"I am constrained in whom I may marry. I have always known that and it was unforgivable of me to forget it. If I led you to believe that I – that we – *sweet Heaven!"*

He turned away, passing his hand over his eyes. His agony was so real that for a moment Elvina could feel only pity for him. Nevertheless her anger was rising as she discerned his meaning.

"You cannot marry me because I do not have a title," she blurted out. "That is what you are saying, isn't it? Mrs. Winters is a lady, but not enough of a lady to marry a Duke."

He turned haggard eyes on her.

"Say what you will. You cannot despise me more than I despise myself."

"But what do you despise yourself for?" she asked bitterly. "For giving your love to me or for lacking the courage of your convictions?"

He winced.

"I deserved that and you have deserved far better from me. You are generous and loving and I have such a poor return to make you. Oh, my dearest, dearest girl, I love you so much. I would give the world if only it was possible for us to marry."

Now was the moment to tell him who she was. When he knew that she was Lady Elvina Winwood, daughter of the Earl Winwood, he would be eager to marry her.

But she could not make herself say the words.

She stared at him, feeling her heart turn to stone.

She had known that the Duke was proud, as his title made inevitable. But she also knew him to be gentle and kindly, and the patrician loftiness that made him reject her as a commoner came as a cruel and brutal surprise.

He loved her, but not enough. That was the plain fact. And if his love was not deep enough to make him defy the world for her, then she wanted none of him.

"I think I hear carriages," she said in a steady voice. "Your first guests are arriving. You should go and receive them."

Then she turned and walked out of the room.

CHAPTER NINE

In the first storm of anger and betrayal Elvina ran to her room and began throwing clothes into a suitcase.

But after a few moments she calmed down and realised that she was acting without thinking.

She could not simply walk out of the house and leave Violet to face the party alone. She had her duties and they must be performed first before she could give vent to her feelings.

Oh, how could this have happened?

How could he have turned out to be so different to what she had believed?

He loved her, but he was determined to set that love aside and make a 'suitable' marriage. In his eyes his duty to his house and lineage was the most important thing in his life. More important than his feelings or hers.

On the face of it, everything was easy. She need only to tell him that she was the daughter of an Earl, he would propose and they would live happily every after.

But they would not.

There could never be peace between them if she knew that he had only married her after she had passed some arcane test of social worthiness.

If he did not love her enough to set the world at nought for her sake, she could never be his wife.

She heard Violet in the corridor and hurried out to her before the girl could enter and see the half-packed case.

"They have started to arrive," Violet cried excitedly.

"Then you must go down and greet the guests at your brother's side," Elvina advised smiling.

She did not know how she managed that smile when her heart was in such turmoil. But tonight she could not think about herself.

Some of her anger died when she saw the Duke. Beneath his smiling manner she could see that he too was devastated by what had happened.

His decision was tearing him apart. But he would force himself to stand by it, nonetheless.

At first the guests were to congregate in the library before making their way to the dining room.

Violet took her place beside her brother. Elvina stayed in the background. She was, after all, only the governess.

Pearson had taken up his position at the library door. As everyone arrived he called out their names and they came forward to greet the Duke and his sister and congratulate him on his birthday.

When the room was almost full Pearson proclaimed,

"The Earl and Countess of Gorleston!"

Through the door came the present Earl of Gorleston, an insignificant creature of middling height and middling appearance. With him was his new wife, who was far from insignificant. One look at the Countess's face told Elvina all she needed to know.

This was a determined young woman, battling her mother-in-law's wishes to continue ruling the roost. From the set of her very firm jaw, she was probably winning. So the Dowager Lady Gorleston had set her heart on marrying her daughter to the Duke and moving into the castle.

"The Dowager Lady Gorleston and Lady Alexandra Gorleston."

The two ladies sailed in together. Lady Alexandra was gorgeously dressed in white satin, sporting the Gorleston diamonds. Her mother was extravagantly splendid in a style that was far too young for her. On her face she wore a look of smug triumph.

Clearly she anticipated victory, guessing that the Duke's pride would ultimately lead him to marry her daughter.

Elvina's heart cried out at the thought. He could never be happy with Lady Alexandra.

And she herself would be faced with years of regret that she had not told him her true identity while there was still time to save them both.

But some core of stubbornness in her told her that this was not the way. If his love was not enough to overcome any obstacle, then they were better apart.

As Lady Gorleston approached the Duke her eyes flickered this way and that. As they briefly alighted on Elvina, standing behind them, the smug look became even more pronounced.

Elvina's unease increased. This woman looked as though she knew something that nobody else knew and was relishing the moment when it would be revealed.

As she reached the Duke she gushed,

"Many, many happy returns, dear David. I have brought you a very special and unusual surprise. Actually it is not really a present for you, but for the young woman who is pretending to teach your sister."

Her voice seemed to ring out, causing many heads to turn.

Now she did not even bother to hide her ill-will.

"I took the liberty of bringing an extra guest, for which I know you will forgive me."

"Of course," the Duke said politely.

"He was particularly anxious to come – for the sake of Mrs. Winters."

Puzzled, the Duke stared at her, and then raised his head to watch the figure coming rather slowly through the door.

Elvina followed his gaze and stiffened.

"Allow me to introduce you," Lady Gorleston resumed, "to Captain Andrew Broadmoor who has been searching for the woman who calls herself Mrs. Winters. *She is actually Lady Elvina Winwood.*"

There was silence.

Everyone looked at Elvina, but the gaze she felt most keenly was the Duke's.

"I do not – understand," he stammered.

"This gentleman is her fiancé," Lady Gorleston trumpeted. "They quarrelled, you know. So unfortunate. But quarrels can be mended and Captain Broadmoor has come hotfoot to reclaim his lady. It is *so* romantic."

Aghast, Elvina studied Andrew, who was looking awkward. As well he might, she thought.

"Mrs. Winters?" the Duke questioned her in a puzzled voice. "Who are you?"

"I am Lady Elvina Winwood," she admitted slowly, "my father was the Earl Winwood."

"Your father – an Earl?"

"Yes. I left my home because I had no further wish to see or speak to Captain Broadmoor. I even changed my identity to avoid him. Far from being my fiancé, he is betrothed to a Miss Margaret Halson."

"No!" Finally Andrew spoke. "There is no betrothal between that lady and me. It was all a misunderstanding."

Elvina turned to face him.

"What happened, Andrew?" she asked. "Is the money spent already? Now you need more, is that it?"

His ashamed look confirmed it, but he added,

"Miss Halson and I decided that we were not suited to each other – "

"Because she has no money?"

"Please," he begged. "I wish I knew why you turned against me so suddenly – "

"Because I overheard you talking to her, planning to jilt her and marry me for my money. That cheque was a goodbye present *and I meant goodbye.*"

He drew in a sharp breath as she made it clear just how much she knew.

But his need for money was too fierce to allow him to give up now.

"Elvina," he said desperately, "if we could only talk privately, I can explain everything."

"There is nothing to explain," she told him. "It's over, Andrew. You must accept that."

"Yes, you must."

Everybody turned, astonished to see who had spoken.

It was Violet and she was looking fiercely determined.

"She does not want to marry you," she told Andrew. "She told me, when she came here, that she had run away from you because you were asking her to marry her when

135

you really loved someone else. That is why she was hiding here from you."

Seeing her plans going awry, Lady Gorleston hurried to say,

"That is not for you, who are only a silly little girl, to decide."

She turned to the Duke.

"If you ask me, your sister's governess, as she calls herself, ought to be very grateful to accept this man, who must love her wildly, *passionately,* since he has come all this way to find her."

There was something unpleasant in the way she spoke.

Then the Duke stepped forward, a stern look on his face and confronted Captain Broadmoor.

"I am afraid your journey has been entirely wasted, sir. This lady cannot marry you, because she is going to marry *me!*"

Uproar!

The Gorleston family looked horrified and Andrew even more so. Violet looked ecstatic and triumphant, while the Duke's expression was tender and delighted.

From the guests came a buzz of pleasure and excitement.

But on Elvina's face there was only consternation.

Her heart was in turmoil. She loved David and wanted to marry him, but not like this.

She had longed for him to love her enough to care nothing for her pedigree. And now it could never happen.

"Your Grace," she murmured, "wait, please."

"Never call me Your Grace again," he said, smiling. "You are my future wife."

"I have not said so."

He smiled again, thinking that he understood her.

"I know, I never asked you properly, did I?" he asked tenderly. "Then I shall ask you now."

"No," she whispered hurriedly. "No, you must not.

Not in front of all these people."

"But I want the world to know that you are to be my wife."

"But perhaps I will not be your wife," she forced herself to say.

"What? What are you saying? Of course we are to be married. Now there is nothing standing in our way."

"You do not understand, do you?" she sighed sadly.

"No, I do not understand. I thought you loved me as much as I love you."

"Do you love me?" she asked wistfully. "I wonder."

"What are you saying?" he murmured, horrified as it began to dawn on him that she was serious.

"We cannot discuss this now," she said hurriedly. "Please, let us just continue with the party."

"But what am I to tell everyone?"

"Say nothing. Let them think what they will, as long as no formal announcement is made. I must deal with Captain Broadmoor."

Without giving him a chance to reply she approached Andrew, who was looking as though he wished the earth would swallow him up.

"Come with me," she ordered firmly.

Grasping his hand, she almost dragged him away and out onto the terrace. There she confronted him. He was looking hopeful again.

"It isn't really over between us, is it?" he pleaded. "You could not bring yourself to marry a great title, because you still love me."

"I do *not* love you, Andrew. I don't think I ever really did. I was lonely. Whatever happened with Margaret?"

"We – decided that we would not suit."

"You mean *you* decided that she didn't have enough money. Was two thousand pounds not enough?"

"It saved me from the worst, but – "

"Oh, give me patience! What did I ever see in you? It is unforgivable of you to come here. How did you know where I was."

"Lady Gorleston came to see me."

"How did she find out?"

"I think she bribed someone in the Duke's stables to keep an eye on Simpson. He sent some letters and this fellow managed to see the address. Then she came to your estate and asked questions until she found me."

"Is Margaret still there?"

"Yes – that is – I think so," he replied lamely.

"You don't know? Are you not concerned about her feelings?"

He gave a helpless shrug.

"What can I do?"

'How could I have imagined myself in love with this paltry creature?' Elvina thought.

"I think you should leave at once, Andrew," she said. "Goodbye."

"But don't you think – ?"

"Goodbye. You had better go down the terrace steps and round to the front. I will explain your absence to Lady Gorleston."

With another miserable shrug he drifted to the steps. Once more he glanced back but, seeing only her implacable face, finally accepted defeat and departed.

At that moment there came a cry from the terrace just above her.

"Where are you?"

"Here," she answered, climbing the steps hastily.

"Thank Heavens!" the Duke called hoarsely. "When I didn't see you I thought you had gone with him."

"Why should I do that? I ran away to escape him in the first place. That is why I came here. I am so sorry I deceived you about my identity but – "

"It doesn't matter," he interrupted her hurriedly. "Violet has told me something of what you confided in her. Mrs. Winters never existed, did she?"

"No. I have never been married. I simply needed another identity in case Andrew came looking for me."

"And Lady Gorleston set herself to find out who you were, because she could sense that I was falling in love with you. *Oh, my darling!*"

On the last words his control broke and he seized her into his arms, raining passionate kisses over her face.

Joy streamed through every part of her and for a blissful moment she yielded. She loved him and she could almost believe that nothing else mattered.

But something stern and almost puritanical in her told her that it was not so easy. It was not enough that he wanted to marry her. It mattered *why*. She could not settle for a flawed love, though her heart broke for him.

"Wait, wait," she told him breathlessly.

"No, my darling, I am not going to wait. I want to go back into that room and tell everyone that you are to be my wife. There are no obstacles standing between us now."

"There never were," she parried quietly.

"But I didn't know that – "

"You knew that we were well suited, that we had similar tastes and I was free to marry. You knew that we loved each other. What more did you need to know?"

"My dear, please, we have talked about this before. I had to consider my duty to my house – "

"Of course and I would not expect you to marry a woman who was not a lady. But I *am* a lady and you knew that, even if you didn't know that I was the social equal of Lady Alexandra.

"I longed for you to set aside pride and position and love me for myself alone. Why, oh, why could you not have done so?"

"Does it matter?" he asked passionately.

"Yes," she replied. "It *does* matter. But we cannot talk about it now. We must return to the party."

There was a step behind them and Violet appeared.

"There you are, you two," she called eagerly. "Do come back. The Gorlestons are furious. We conquered them! Isn't it fun? Now we can tell everyone."

"Yes, we must go inside," the Duke said in a strained voice. "But we will make no announcements tonight."

"Oh, David, don't be such a stick-in-the-mud! Who cares whether you announce it in *The Times* first?"

But something in his pale face made her fall silent.

Quietly the Duke drew his sister's arm through his.

"Come," he said. "We must see to our guests."

All eyes were on them when they returned to the library and the curiosity intensified when they saw that Andrew was no longer with them.

But the Duke played his part to perfection. His smiles concealed the blow he had just received, and nothing could have exceeded his amiability as he ushered his guests into the dining room.

Nor could anything have exceeded the firmness with which he refused to notice the entire Gorleston family glaring at him. Even the normally supine Lady Alexandra was roused to a glance of hostility, as though she sensed that her chance had gone, but did not quite know why.

Her mother knew why, as her eyes directed at Elvina made clear. But Elvina followed the Duke's example and refused to notice her.

Somehow they all struggled through the evening until it was time for the guests to leave. Lady Gorleston departed with a toss of her head.

"Well done," the Duke said quietly to Violet. "You managed your first grown-up party beautifully. You are a credit to Mrs. – to Lady Elvina."

"Fancy her having a title all the time."

"Yes, fancy," the Duke agreed in a wan voice.

"We should have guessed," Violet continued. "I mean it was obvious really."

"It was obvious that she was a woman of means. You had only to see her horses."

"No, I mean more than that. It doesn't matter whether she has a title or not. It is a certain *something* about her."

"Yes," he agreed in a tense voice. "By the way, where is she?"

"She went upstairs. She said she was tired."

"You had better look in and see if she's all right. Goodnight, my dear."

They kissed each other and Violet hurried upstairs.

She knocked on Elvina's room and entered without waiting for an answer.

"Mrs. Winters – oh, no! I must call you Lady Elvina now, mustn't I? Why, what are you doing?"

Appalled, she stared at the open suitcase on Elvina's bed, which was gradually filling with clothes.

"I am getting ready to leave," Elvina said. "I cannot stay here any longer."

"But why? I thought that you and David – you know."

"That was an illusion – it can never be and you must not even think about it."

Violet would have argued, but something in Elvina's demeanour that she had not seen before, made her stop.

The next moment she had darted out of the room. Running downstairs, she burst into the library where her brother was sitting by the fire.

"She's going," she screamed. "She is packing her things because she says she cannot stay here any longer. David you must stop her."

"She won't listen to me," he said sombrely. "I have offended her too dreadfully."

"Oh, stuff! How could you offend her?"

"That's what I am still trying to understand myself.

142

But she is so angry with me."

"But it's just a lover's tiff, whatever she says."

"Why, what has she said?"

"I asked her about you and she and she said it was an illusion and that it could never be."

He had half risen, but now he sank back in his chair and the light disappeared from his face.

"Go to bed, Violet."

"But David, aren't you even going to try?"

"Go to bed, my dear."

She left him, but turned at the door for a last look. He sat with his head sunk, staring into the fire and at last she crept away.

The Duke stayed as he was for an hour. Then he rose and walked out onto the stone terrace, looking at the grounds shining in the light of the moon.

A figure, huddled in a cloak, was walking across the lawn. At the bottom of the steps she stopped and looked up at him.

He came slowly down to her.

"Violet says you are leaving."

"Yes, Simpson and I will go first thing tomorrow."

"Is there nothing I can say to make you stay with me all my life?"

Sadly she shook her head.

"I do not want to go but I cannot help myself. What I feel is too strong for me to go against it. I suppose that makes me like you, really."

"Don't," he said, closing his eyes and wincing.

"I am sorry. I didn't mean that cruelly. It's just that in a way I understand. What you were reared to believe in stays with you all your life."

"What were *you* reared to believe in?" he asked, almost as though he was afraid of the answer.

"Love," she replied simply. "I saw my parents' love for each other and it seemed to fill the world. As I grew up I had only one dream – to find a love like theirs.

"I knew that when the time came for me to marry, it would be because the man and I loved each other as my parents did, so totally that nothing else mattered.

"I thought I had found that kind of love in Captain Broadmoor, until I discovered that he was pursuing me for my money, while secretly loving another woman."

She sighed as she continued,

"Maybe I am being unrealistic because how many couples are like my parents? I only know that I cannot settle for less."

"And I would not offer you less," he pleaded. "You are the only woman who will ever live in my heart."

"Yes, now that you know the truth about me. If only you had not learned it like this."

"It's done now and cannot be helped. I love you – worship you. I think of you, dream of you night and day. We are made for each other. Haven't you felt that?"

"Yes," she cried in agony. "I have felt it many times, but I was deluding myself. If you could love me and marry Lady Alexandra – "

"I could never have married her," he interrupted fiercely.

"But why not?" she hurled at him, made angry by her misery. "She is an Earl's daughter and your social equal –

almost. Not quite, of course, but I suppose even a Duke has to look a little beneath him for a wife."

"Stop it," he said intensely, seizing her by the shoulders and giving her a shake. "Don't talk like that, I forbid you."

"As Your Grace commands," she responded with bitter irony.

"I said stop it! How dare you talk that way when you know that I love you, *that we love each other?*"

"Do we?" she flung at him. "I wonder."

He stared at her, his hands still gripping her shoulders tightly.

Then with a growl of *"let's put an end to this nonsense!"* he pulled her against him.

He kissed her fervently with a driving passion that almost overwhelmed her. In a moment he had blotted out the world, leaving only the two of them in the fire of their mutual desire.

Elvina kissed him back. She could not help herself. But even while she yielded to her feelings, an independent voice in her head vowed that she would not be overwhelmed against her better judgement.

"You love me," he murmured against her mouth. "Say it."

"I love you," she gasped.

"Nothing else matters. We will be married as soon as possible."

"No!"

"I say *yes* and I will not be refused. Do you think I am going to let you go?"

Elvina freed herself and spoke in a fury.

"You have no choice. How dare you try to order me about! I am neither slave nor servant, but a free woman and I say *no*. I wouldn't let Andrew lord it over me and I will not allow you!"

There was a moment's freezing silence, during which he stared into her face. Now he too was angry, his eyes hard and glittering.

Then he released her and stepped back.

"Very well! Have it as you wish. I do not understand you and I will not pretend to. If you are set on destroying us both there is no more to be said."

"You are right," she said quietly. "There is no more to be said."

"I will order the carriage ready to take you to the station tomorrow."

He inclined his head to her sharply.

"Goodnight to you, madam."

She stood where she was as he walked away from her across the lawn. She felt drained and exhausted and there was a terrible ache in her heart.

*

She was in the stables at dawn next morning to speak to Simpson and give him money and instructions for taking Mars and Jupiter home. Violet was waiting for her in the breakfast room, but there was no sign of the Duke, which was a relief or so she told herself.

"I cannot believe that you are really going," Violet spluttered tearfully. "Please don't. It will be so terrible without you."

"I have no choice, my dear," Elvina replied sadly. "I cannot marry your brother. It could never have worked out."

Violet was about to burst out in protestations, but something about Elvina's pale face silenced her.

Elvina drank her coffee, wondering when the Duke would appear to say goodbye to her. But after a while she faced the fact that he was not coming.

He was going to let her leave without a word.

When that realisation came to her, she raised her chin. If that was how things were, so be it.

The time had come. She kissed Violet goodbye and walked out to the waiting carriage, a small closed vehicle. The coachman was ready on the box. A footman opened the door and handed her in.

Then, just as the door closed, the far door opened and someone jumped in quickly as the carriage began to move.

"Good morning," said the Duke.

Her heart overflowed with relief. Now he would take her into his arms and perhaps, somehow, they would find a second chance.

But all he said was,

"I thought I would escort you at least part of the way to the station."

"And make sure that I really departed?" she asked lightly.

"Perhaps. I spent a sleepless night thinking over what you said and now I know that you are right. How could we make it a happy marriage when neither of us will soften and try to understand the other?

"You told me that you had grown up believing in love above all else. You said you could not swerve from that

147

belief because you had been raised to it and it was a part of you.

"And yet you judged me because I clung to the beliefs in which I was reared. Perhaps it was wrong of me to place the dignity of my house and the pride of lineage so high, but that was what I was taught to do.

"In time, you might have taught me better. But now we will never know."

Elvina stared at him, her face white with shock as she realised the truth of his words.

"You are right to leave me," he said. "We had our chance, but we lost it."

He raised her hand and brushed his lips against it.

"Goodbye, my dearest. I will never forget you and what might have been."

He rapped against the wall of the carriage and the vehicle stopped. The Duke opened the door, climbed down into the road, closing the door behind him.

"Drive on," he called to the coachman.

The carriage began to move.

With tears pouring down her face, Elvina turned to look through the small rear window. Through it she could see the road stretching away from whence she had come, and the Duke, who had already turned and was walking along it away from her.

His head was down and his shoulders hunched as if in despair, but his step never wavered and he did not look back.

She watched until the last moment, as he grew smaller and smaller, until he vanished among the trees leaving only emptiness behind.

CHAPTER TEN

After two days Simpson arrived home with the horses, and Elvina hurried out to the stables to meet them. She hugged Jupiter and Mars again and again, burying her face against their satin necks.

The servants were agog, eager to know from Simpson why their Mistress had returned, pale and distraught, without a word to say to anyone. But Simpson was tight-lipped, which only served to increase the speculation.

Elvina had been dreading a meeting with Margaret, which could only be awkward for both of them. But Margaret had departed, leaving a forwarding address for her belongings.

Elvina despatched them with a generous cheque. She bore Margaret no ill-will.

But it meant that now she was alone with nothing to do in the evenings but sit and brood.

The Duke's words had struck her like a blow.

It was all true.

She had blamed him for instinctively doing what he had been reared to do and yet she had done the same. He had implied that with time and enough love, she could have taught him a better way. *And it was true*.

Instead she had made one swift cruel judgement and given him no chance to make amends.

Now it was she who could never make amends. It was all over between them and nothing could put it right.

She gave Jupiter and Mars time to rest after their journey home and then she began taking them out and spending all day on horseback, first Jupiter, then Mars, next Jupiter and then Mars again.

One day as she was riding home in the gloom she saw a small commotion as soon as she came within sight of the house. Her housekeeper had come out onto the front porch and stood waiting for her with every sign of urgency. As Elvina slowed, the housekeeper ran a few steps towards her.

"Oh, thank Heavens you're back, my lady! Such a thing has happened and none of us knows what to do. She says she must see you and won't go away until she has, and she won't go back in any case because she's run away forever and – "

"Mrs. Jenkins, whatever are you talking about?"

Elvina asked, dismounting and handing the reins to a groom.

"Who is here?"

"Lady Violet Castleforde, my Lady."

"What?"

"She arrived an hour ago, my Lady, with her maid."

"Thank goodness for that! Where are they?"

"In the library. I have taken them some supper and prepared rooms. I hope I did the right thing."

"Absolutely right. We cannot send Lady Violet back at this hour."

She hurried inside, her mind in a whirl at this latest development. As Mrs. Jenkins had said, she found Violet in the library, accompanied by the maid who had looked after them both at the castle.

As soon as she saw Elvina, Violet cast herself upon her.

"Oh, Elvina, I am so glad you are here. I won't go back, please don't say I have to. I hate it."

"Calm down," she soothed.

"I won't go back to the castle. I hate it now you are not there."

"All right, we will talk later once you are settled in. I am glad you had the sense to bring your maid."

It soon became apparent that Violet had organised her departure very well. She had brought a large amount of luggage, which the maid was soon despatched to unpack.

"And now tell me everything," Elvina said once they were alone. "Whatever are you doing here? You cannot just run away."

"I can and I have! The castle is hateful now you have gone."

"But your brother will be worried out of his mind. What must he be thinking right now?"

"He doesn't know anything yet. He has gone away for a few days."

"And he will come back and find you gone. Oh, Heavens!"

"I left him a letter saying I could no longer endure living with a brother who is permanently in an evil temper."

"I am sure that is an exaggeration."

"It isn't. Since you left he slouches around the castle, looking grim and nobody dares to talk to him."

"Is he really that angry?"

"Angry? He's wretched, *miserable*. He cannot bear to talk to anyone."

"I do not think so, Violet. He is just very angry with me. He told me so when I left."

151

"Well, he's not angry now, not with you, anyway. Just everyone else. It's like living under a black cloud, so I left!"

"Then I must write to him and explain where you are."

"Oh, please don't send me away," Violet begged piteously.

"That is up to him. I will tell him that you are welcome to stay here and perhaps he will agree."

"Do you think he will?" Violet asked touchingly.

"I shall tell him that it will benefit your education to spend more time with your governess," Elvina said firmly.

She waited until everyone was in bed before sitting down later that night to write the hardest letter of her life.

She tried to set aside the picture Violet had given her of the Duke sunk in despair. Violet was a romantic girl, who thought it would be easy to reunite two lovers.

But it could not be easy when there was pride, obstinacy and bitterness on both sides.

At last Elvina settled for a formal tone.

'My Lord Duke,

I have to report the safe arrival of Lady Violet who has asked to remain with me for a while. As I believe her education would benefit from time spent with me, I am requesting your permission for her to stay.

I feel sure I do not need to assure you that Lady Violet will be well cared for in my household at all times.

I hope to hear from you very soon.

Yours sincerely,

Elvina Winwood.'

She tried to remain detached as she sealed the letter, but she could not banish from her mind the thought of him receiving the letter, the look on his face as he saw that it was from her.

Perhaps he would come here himself. She would see him again. They would soften to each other and somehow find a way forward.

Anything would be better than this wretched loneliness, thinking of him night and day, becoming increasingly sure that she had made the wrong decision.

But perhaps he was feeling the same and would seize this opportunity to come to her.

She had only a short time to wait for her answer, which came by return of post. It was a letter, not from the Duke, but from his secretary.

'My Lady,

His Grace has asked me to convey to you his thanks for your hospitality to the Lady Violet, and his agreement to her residing with you for the immediate future.

I remain your Ladyship's obedient servant,
John Kenham.'

It was like a blow over the heart. He could not have told her more clearly that he was finished with her, as she had declared she was with him.

She could not blame him for accepting her decision.

Her heart was breaking, but she would be strong, learn to live with reality and devote herself to Violet. The girl had learned to trust her and she would not betray that trust.

"We have to look forward to next year," she told her, "when you will make you debut at a great ball at Castleforde House in London. "You will be gorgeous in white satin and no other *debutante* will hold a candle to you. You will wear the Castleforde pearls – "

153

"No, the Castleforde diamonds," Violet broke in eagerly.

"Pearls," Elvina said firmly. "Diamonds are too old for you. You may wear them after you are married."

Violet pulled a face, but instantly she was smiling again and saying,

"Tell me all about when you were a *debutante*."

Elvina reminisced about her own coming out ball, which now seemed so very distant.

"Did you have lots of admirers?" Violet wanted to know?

"Lots," Elvina replied. "But none of them was the right one. I knew that even then."

"How do you know when the man is *the one*?"

"Sometimes you don't, not at first." Elvina gave a sigh. "It's fatally easy to get it wrong."

"You mean like you and David?" Violet asked.

"I think it is time for you to go to bed now," Elvina suggested hastily.

While the weather was still warm she took Violet on expeditions to visit the locality. Once they travelled to the seaside and stayed for four days.

On their return there was a letter for Violet in handwriting that Elvina recognised as the Duke's. Before her heart had time to skip a beat, Violet had whisked it away and hurried upstairs.

When she came down for dinner she did not mention the contents to Elvina.

*

The year was moving on and the colours were turning to the tints of autumn.

The Times reported that Queen Victoria had made her annual visit to Balmoral in Scotland and would be attending the Highland games at Braemar.

"David usually goes to Scotland," Violet confided one afternoon as they were shopping in Elswick. "The Queen is very fond of him. She says she likes to see him in a kilt because he has such good legs."

"Really?" Elvina said, trying to sound indifferent. "And is he going this year?"

"Oh, yes," Violet said airily. "He must be there by now."

Through the newspapers Elvina was able to follow the Queen's stay in Scotland, but although she read every line several times she was unable to find any mention of the Duke of Castleforde.

Then the Queen left Scotland and she ceased to follow the newspaper reports.

"I suppose, Violet, you ought to return to your brother one day soon," she said one evening.

"Why don't you come with me?" Violet asked. "I am sure he would like to see you."

"I don't think so. He didn't even answer my letter. He just arranged for his secretary to write to me."

"Of course, he would die rather than write to you himself," Violet commented wisely. "He is much too proud. Isn't that silly of him?"

"Very silly," Elvina agreed. "But then, I was silly and proud too. I lost my temper. My father always said I was too hasty, especially when I became angry and didn't think properly."

"What exactly *did* you quarrel about?" Violet wanted to know.

"He didn't tell you?"

"He said you were stubborn and unforgiving, which was a very strange thing for him to say."

"Why was it strange? I was stubborn and unforgiving."

"You do not understand. Castlefordes can do no wrong. It's a matter of family pride. And if you do no wrong, you don't think you need forgiveness. It must be the first time David has ever admitted that he needed to be forgiven for anything."

"Yes, I see. Nothing else?"

"No, he just broods about how 'unkindly' you judged him."

"I was upset because he was not going to marry me before he discovered I was an Earl's daughter. When he knew that I had the correct social standing, he asked me at once."

"That is disgraceful!" Violet said, horrified. "As though anything mattered but your love. He should be boiled in oil!"

"That is just what I thought at first, but it wasn't really his fault. He instinctively read the situation as he had been reared to react. But so did I. I thought he should put love first, because that was how *I* was reared."

"But you were right and he was wrong," Violet asserted stubbornly.

"I was raised surrounded by love. Your brother wasn't. Should he be blamed because he didn't understand its ways or its importance? He could have learned about love through me, if I had been more generous."

"I still think he should be boiled in oil. He is not worthy of you and you are better off without him!"

Elvina sighed.

"No," she said. "I will never be better off without him. I made a cruel mistake and now it's too late."

Violet, who was sitting on a stool beside Elvina's chair, looked up at her.

"Are you sure it's too late?" she questioned earnestly.

"He will never forgive me. He as good as told me so when we parted."

"But perhaps he is sorry too."

"Then why doesn't he come and see me and say so?"

"Because he is too proud," Violet explained. "And that brings us back to where we started!"

She spoke kindly and patiently, as though talking to someone unusually slow-witted and Elvina had a strange feeling that something was happening that she did not understand.

When she had bade Violet goodnight and gone to her own room, Elvina lay in bed, tossing and turning. The conversation had disturbed her.

'Perhaps he's sorry too.'

The words echoed in her heart.

'He won't say sorry because he is too proud.'

'And I have been too proud,' Elvina pondered. 'But one of us has to make it right or we will lose each other for ever.

'And I will not let that happen.'

On that thought she fell asleep and enjoyed her best night since she had left the castle.

She rose quietly at dawn and scribbled a quick letter to Violet, which she slipped under her door. Then she crept downstairs and ran to the stables.

There she woke Simpson by throwing a stone at his window. Twenty minutes later he was driving her to Kelnwich station in the dogcart.

*

It was two hours before Simpson returned home to be met by an agitated Violet.

"Did you take Lady Elvina to the station?" she demanded anxiously.

"Yes, my Lady."

"Did she actually catch the train?"

"Yes, my Lady. I actually saw her Ladyship onto the train and watched it depart."

"*Ooooh!*" Violet wailed desperately.

"Her Ladyship did say that she had left you a letter, explaining everything."

"Yes, she did. That's what is so terrible!"

Simpson did not point out the illogicality of this last remark. Or perhaps he knew more than he admitted.

"As soon as I have had breakfast I want to go into Kelnwich."

"Yes, my Lady."

An hour later, both refreshed, they met up again and he drove her into the little town.

"*The Prince Regent Hotel,*" she said, naming the best hotel in town.

As soon as they reached the hotel she jumped down and hurried inside, running to the desk and saying breathlessly,

"I have come to see Mr. Baines. I know he is in room fifteen, so if you will please tell me where it is – ?"

The porter looked horrified at the thought of a well-bred young lady going unchaperoned to a gentleman's room.

"On the second floor, miss, but wouldn't it be better if I sent for – ?"

"No, no, it's all right," she called over her shoulder as she ran up the stairs. "He's my brother."

A moment later she was knocking on the door of room fifteen. It opened and she hurled herself into the arms of 'Mr. Baines'.

"Oh, David, something terrible has happened. It's all gone wrong!"

"Come, it cannot be as bad as that," the Duke replied, although he had gone a little pale. "What's happened? Has that Broadmoor fellow turned up again?"

"Oh, no, and it wouldn't matter if he had. She doesn't love him, *she loves you*. She told me so last night!"

A glow of delight suffused his face, which had grown haggard and drawn over the last few weeks.

"That's wonderful," he sighed. "Does she know that I am here?"

"No, she thinks you are at the castle. As I told you in my first letter, I did it just as we planned. I turned up on her doorstep and told her I had run away because you were so horrible that nobody could bear to live with you – "

"Yes, I can imagine. I am sure you enjoyed that bit!"

"I did. And I was really, really convincing. Tears and everything."

"In other words, you thoroughly enjoyed yourself," he added wryly.

"I did exactly what you told me to do," she replied with offended dignity. "And Elvina has never once suspected that we planned the whole operation together."

"I know. Your letters have been very illuminating. You have done wonderfully well as my ambassador and now it seems that together we will succeed. So what can have gone wrong?"

"Everything!" Violet exclaimed tragically. "When I got up this morning, Elvina had gone and she left me this letter."

She handed him the note she had found pushed under her door that morning.

'Violet dear,

I have been thinking over what we said last night, and I have decided that the only way is for me to go and see your brother, to try to put matters right.

By the time you read this letter I shall be on my way to the castle. Since I started early I shall probably be back tonight. If not, tomorrow morning. Do not worry.

Cross your fingers for me,

Elvina.'

"What are we going to do?" Violet wailed.

"I rather think that I am going to be married?" he answered with a faint smile. "And it is all thanks to you and your excellent work on my behalf."

"But she will arrive at the castle and find that you are not there."

"So she will come back home. Of course, she will be breathing fire at both of us for deceiving her, so we will need to endure her wrath – "

"*You* can endure her wrath. It was all your idea."

"The point is that she will be here."

160

"But shouldn't we go in hot pursuit?"

"My dear girl, she has several hours start on us. We would pass each other in two trains going in opposite directions. It makes more sense for us to stay here on the station for when her train pulls in."

"But that could be late tonight or tomorrow."

"Then I am prepared to settle in for a long wait. I do not care how long it is so long as I find her at the end of it."

"*We'll* settle in for a wait," Violet said. "I am coming with you."

"But it could be hours and hours – "

"We are in this together," she declared firmly.

"Yes, indeed we are. Together then."

*

It was early afternoon when Elvina reached the castle. "I have come to see the Duke," she told Pearson. "Can you take me to him, please?"

The butler looked bewildered.

"But my Lady, I understood – that is – Kelnwich is surely close to Winwood Grange?"

"Yes, it is just down the road from my home," she agreed, bewildered. "But what does that have to do with anything?"

"His Grace is at Kelnwich."

"His Grace is what?"

"For the last few weeks he has been staying at the *Prince Regent Hotel* in Kelnwich."

Elvina stared at him.

"Are you quite certain of that?"

"All his mail is forwarded there, my Lady."

Elvina ignored the voice buzzing in her head and pulled herself together.

"What about the Braemar Games?" she asked.

"His Grace did not visit Scotland this year."

"Do you happen to recall exactly when he went to Kelnwich?"

"Oh, yes, my Lady. It was a week after you left. The Duke and Lady Violet departed together. The head groom took them to the railway station and saw then onto the train to Derby."

"They *both* caught the train to Derby?" Elvina asked slowly. "And from there they caught the connection to Kelnwich."

"As to that, I could not say, my Lady. But they certainly caught the Derby train together. Lady Violet's maid was with them too."

"Of course she was," Elvina murmured. "It was all so beautifully organised."

"May I fetch your Ladyship a cup of tea?"

"Thank you. I feel in need of one. And perhaps you could arrange for me to be driven back to Arnside station, since I have sent my cab away?"

She reached Arnside just in time to miss a train. There was nothing to do but sit on the platform and wait for the next one, which gave her two hours to mull over the way she had been fooled.

It was so obvious now that they had planned it together. *Violet had not run away at all.*

'He came all the way to Kelnwich with her,' she thought, 'and he stayed at the local hotel while she came on to my home and gave me a pathetic tale of how she had been forced to flee him.

'And she has been in touch with him all this time, probably telling him every word I have said.'

But why?

Why?

'And all those things she said about how he should be boiled in oil and he wasn't worthy of me!' Why?

She was still asking herself that question when the Derby train came in and she boarded it. By now it was getting late in the evening and it would be after midnight before the train reached Kelnwich.

She sat staring out of the windows at the darkness, trying not to admit to herself what she knew to be true.

He had come after her. He wanted her back. Too proud to plead for himself, he had engaged Violet as his ambassador. Violet was to ascertain Elvina's state of mind and contact him if she detected any sign of softening.

It had all been a plot to win her back, because he loved her as much as she loved him, but did not know how to say so.

That was the blazing, glorious truth and her heart swelled at the realisation.

If only the train would move faster! But of course, it was too late for today. When she reached the station she would have to return home and try to be patient until the next morning.

Or perhaps he would be waiting for her at home, because Violet must have taken her letter to him.

Or perhaps –

But that was too much to hope for.

The train was slowing. She was nearly there. Suddenly her heart was racing.

She could endure the uncertainty no longer. Pushing down the window, she looked out, fixing her gaze on the platform coming closer and closer.

In the smoky gloom she could not be sure of anything. He was there. He was not there.

Then the smoke cleared and she saw him, standing on the platform, wearing a look of anxiety that matched her own – anxiety that turned to a blazing smile as soon as he saw her.

And there was Violet beside him, jumping up and down with excitement and waving.

But as the train drew to a halt Violet backed away, leaving her brother standing alone, his heart in his eyes.

He ran forward, pulling open the door and opening his arms so that Elvina fell straight into them. He lowered his head and for a long moment neither of them moved.

"Can you forgive me for being such a hidebound fool?" he asked at last in a husky voice. "I deserve to lose you for not appreciating the priceless jewel I was given, but please don't tell me that I have lost *you*, because I could not bear it."

"I could never bear to leave you again for even one second," she told him, her eyes shining. "I love you with all my heart."

"With all *my* heart," he echoed, "and all *my* soul, and all *my* life. You are mine for eternity and I will never, never let you go. Say that you will always be mine."

"How can I not be yours, when you went to such lengths?" she asked, laughing through her tears. "Such a wild, incredible plan! Violet had me completely fooled."

"You see, I always knew I could be an actress," Violet carolled triumphantly. "You didn't suspect anything, did you?"

"Not for a moment."

"But it was David's idea. He planned the whole scheme."

"*You*?" She stared at him.

"You see, I am learning already," he admitted.

The guard's whistle blew. The train began to move again.

"My bag, it's still on the train!" Elvina cried.

"No, it isn't." Violet held it up. "I collected it and shut the door while you two were 'otherwise occupied'. Now, it's late and cold and we have a wedding to plan. So can we please go home?"

The Duke looked down into Elvina's face and his arms tightened about her, as hers did around him.

"We *are* home, forever and always," he sighed.

"We are the most fortunate souls in the whole wide world. We have at last found our way to Heaven."

Printed in Poland
by Amazon Fulfillment
Poland Sp. z o.o., Wrocław